SWEET KISS

"May I say you wade most charmingly? This cannot be your first attempt," Damon stated.

"Thank you, 'tis not," Ashley said primly. "Though always before, I waded alone."

"Do you not find, like the waltz, 'tis more agreeable with a companion?"

"I cannot compare the two, sir, since I have never waltzed."

"When the happy occasion occurs, I can only hope to be your first partner. Perhaps you will do me the honor at a country dance or mayhap in London. I trust the time will be soon."

"Alas, I fear there will never be such a time."

"Pray, do not say so, for you doom me to eternal misery."

"No," she murmured. "If anyone is doomed, I am." To his utmost surprise, she pulled free of his grasp, covered her face with her hands and burst into tears.

Damon put an arm around her. She leaned her head against his chest and cried as though her heart would break. Few events left Damon at a loss, but this was one of them. "If I can help you in any way, I shall be glad to."

Gazing at Damon, Ashley blinked back new tears. "No one can help me."

Damon watched Ashley nibble at her luscious lower lip and was undone. Cupping her face in his hands, he kissed her, gently at first, then, when she didn't push away, more urgently . . .

WATCH FOR THESE ZEBRA REGENCIES

LADY STEPHANIE   (0-8217-5341-X, $4.50)
by Jeanne Savery
Lady Stephanie Morris has only one true love: the family estate she has
managed ever since her mother died. But then Lord Anthony Rider
arrives on her estate, claiming he has plans for both the land and the
woman. Stephanie soon realizes she's fallen in love with a man whose
sensual caresses will plunge her into a world of peril and intrigue . . .
a man as dangerous as he is irresistible.

BRIGHTON BEAUTY   (0-8217-5340-1, $4.50)
by Marilyn Clay
Chelsea Grant, pretty and poor, naively takes school friend Alayna
Marchmont's place and spends a month in the country. The devastating
man had sailed from Honduras to claim his promised bride, Miss
Marchmont. An affair of the heart may lead to disaster . . . unless a
resourceful Brighton beauty finds a way to stop a masquerade and keep
a lord's love.

LORD DIABLO'S DEMISE   (0-8217-5338-X, $4.50)
by Meg-Lynn Roberts
The sinfully handsome Lord Harry Glendower was a gambler and the
black sheep of his family. About to be forced into a marriage of con-
venience, the devilish fellow engineered his own demise, never having
dreamed that faking his death would lead him to the heavenly refuge
of spirited heiress Gwyn Morgan, the daughter of a physician.

A PERILOUS ATTRACTION   (0-8217-5339-8, $4.50)
by Dawn Aldridge Poore
Alissa Morgan is stunned when a frantic passenger thrusts her baby into
Alissa's arms and flees, having heard rumors that a notorious highwayman posed a threat to their coach. Handsome stranger Hugh Sebastian
secretly possesses the treasured necklace the highwayman seeks and
volunteers to pose as Alissa's husband to save her reputation. With a
lost baby and missing necklace in their care, the couple embarks on a
journey into peril—and passion.

*Available wherever paperbacks are sold, or order direct from the
Publisher. Send cover price plus 50¢ per copy for mailing and
handling to Penguin USA, P.O. Box 999, c/o Dept. 17109, Ber-
genfield, NJ 07621. Residents of New York and Tennessee must
include sales tax. DO NOT SEND CASH.*

A Deceptive Bequest

Olivia Sumner

ZEBRA BOOKS
KENSINGTON PUBLISHING CORP.

ZEBRA BOOKS are published by

Kensington Publishing Corp.
850 Third Avenue
New York, NY 10022

Zebra and the Z logo Reg. U.S. Pat. & TM Off.

First Printing: August, 1996
10 9 8 7 6 5 4 3 2 1

Printed in the United States of America

One

The rowboat was gone.

Ashley Douglas searched along the riverbank above and below the brook inlet where Mr. Graham was in the habit of leaving the boat drawn up on the shore. As she searched, she felt the prickling in her thumbs that presaged a change.

Could the missing boat be an omen? Ever since she was a child, Ashley had believed the time would come when the mystery of her birth would be no more and the identity of her mother and father revealed so she could assume her rightful place in the world, whatever that might be. Yet each time, the change that occurred after her thumbs began to prick had been something other than her longed-for dream.

Still she clung to her hope that her lot in life was meant to be more than marriage to one of the young men who dangled after her or to one of the respectable widowers who had offered for her. She had, she knew, already tried the Grahams' patience with her refusals and could not expect to do so much longer. As Mrs. Graham had pointed out less than a fortnight ago, young ladies of nearly twenty with no expectations should not be so choosy.

So she prayed the missing boat might prove to be the omen of a wonderful change in her fortunes. But whether it was an omen or not, the boat was nowhere to be found, and without the boat she would have to walk more than a mile upstream to Mitred Bridge and then the same distance down the other bank of Dane's Run, losing an hour's time in all. Hardly a promising beginning for the day, especially since she had so little time to call her own.

"Waste not, want not," Ashley reminded herself as she set off briskly along the path at the top of the riverbank, determined not to give up her few precious hours in the glen. The summer before she had discovered the secret pool in this wooded refuge, a glen carved by Dane's Run before the river had changed course at some forgotten time in the past. No one she had asked seemed certain when that had been, though surely long before she came to live with the Grahams and undoubtedly many years before her birth.

Thinking once more about her birth caused her pace to slow, and she sighed, then shook her head. She had little cause to feel sorry for herself; the Grahams were kind enough to her, in their way. A family who took in an orphan had a perfect right to expect that she would make herself useful to them. Did not the Grahams provide her with food and clothes and a place to sleep? In truth, though she worked hard, she was not treated as a servant. Many orphans were far less fortunate than she, as the Reverend Mr. Mills was wont to remind her time and again. But she never lost her dream of being loved and cherished by someone she truly belonged to.

With an effort, she dismissed her impossible fantasy. Though she had little enough to call her own, these next two hours were hers, precious jewels to enjoy. The warmth of the sun on her shoulders, the fresh May green of the fields and woods, and the bubbling rush of the river soon brought a smile to her face. After three days of rain, how wonderful to be out in the sunshine.

But where was the boat? The rains had muddied and swollen Dane's Run, yet she doubted the river had risen enough to float the Graham rowboat free. And Mr. Graham, a firm believer that one should neither a borrower nor a lender be, would not have lent his boat to anyone.

A half-hour later, she neared the first bend in the river. Before she reached it, men's shouts and laughter rode the breeze around the curve and she paused to listen, a certainty forming in her mind. For the last two days carriages had rumbled through the nearby village of Louth on their way from London to the Mitred manor house. One of those visitors might well have taken the boat as a prank; young men of the *ton* were great ones for hums, as they called them, and wouldn't think twice about "borrowing" a rowboat beached along a country stream.

"Mind you, those elegant London gentlemen don't think of it as stealing," Mrs. Graham had said, in reference to a wheelbarrow gone missing after the last manor house party. " 'Tis stealing all the same, whatever word they may use in the city. I do hope you remember to heed my warning to keep well out of the way of such high-flyers. They have no more respect for country maidens than they do for country property."

Ashley did not doubt Mrs. Graham was quite correct. On the other hand, the carefree manners of the London visitors fascinated her. From afar, that is. She would not care to have a close encounter with any gentleman of the *ton*.

The male voices grew louder—no more than two of them, she decided, and definitely not locals. Ashley hesitated, poised to flee, while a frisson of fear mixed with excitement coursed along her spine. Not far ahead lay the single span of the stone bridge crossing Dane's Run. If she hurried, she might be able to dash over it before the gentlemen rounded the bend. If she reached the cover of the trees on the opposite side, she would be hidden from observation while she spied on their antics. Furthermore, she might discover whether or not they had actually taken Mr. Graham's boat.

Squire Mitred and his visitors from London belonged to another world, a world she could scarcely imagine, a world of many servants and fine carriages, of ballrooms and fashionable clothes, its inhabitants as foreign to her as the Turkish sultans or the Chinese emperors the reverend's wife had taught her about. Not that any gentleman from London had any right to set himself above Ashley Douglas, she told herself. After all, she did not spend her life in idleness and debauchery, as Mr. Mills implied members of the *ton* were wont to do.

Ashley glanced down at her gown, a blue-sprigged calico with an unmodishly low waistline and a high neck, plain and serviceable. She settled her straw bonnet more firmly on her bound-back auburn hair and then studied her ungloved chapped hands. No one would ever mistake her for a member of the *ton!*

The prow of a boat poking around the bend brought her up short. *Rats and mice!* as Freddie the stableboy had taken to saying, after Mrs. Graham had severely chastised him for using language unfit for a lady's ears. Her lollygagging had caused her to miss the chance to cross the bridge; neither did she have time to retreat along the path. Quickly examining the meager growth of bushes on her side of the river, she decided the cover was not enough to conceal so much as a rabbit.

Ashley took a deep, apprehensive breath as she tried to convince herself that facing down gentlemen from London would be no more difficult than discouraging local would-be swains. She fixed her gaze on the boat sweeping around the curve and noticed something floating in the rushing water well ahead of the boat. An oar? No, two. Both oars. And yes, it was Mr. Graham's boat. Anger began to simmer within her—not only had they appropriated the boat without asking, they were lack-witted enough to lose the oars.

A man with wildly disordered blond hair rounded the bend, staggering along the path toward her, arms semaphoring, his attention all on the boat, which was almost even with her.

"Damon!" he shouted. "Watch it, man, the bloody thing's tipping."

Ashley watched in disbelief as the boat rolled over, flinging its occupant into the swollen waters of Dane's Run. Bottom up it swept past her while a dark-haired man floundered about in the river. Serves him right to get his fine clothes soaked, she thought. But as she stared at him, she belatedly realized that deep as Dane's Run was from the rains, if he could not swim, he might well be drowning.

The blond man fell to his knees near her, stretching a hand toward the one struggling in the water. Instead of making an effort to reach the bank, the man called Damon sank like a cast-off sad iron.

"Can he swim?" she cried.

"Damme 'f I know," the kneeling man answered. "*I* can't swim a stroke. 'M like a cat. Hate water."

Listening to his slurred words, she understood he had been overindulging. No doubt Damon was also foxed, which would account for his overturning the boat.

Drunk or sober, she could not allow him to drown right before her eyes. Thanking God that she had learned to swim after a fashion by secretly observing Freddie paddling in the river and then imitating his actions when she was alone in her secret pool in the glen, Ashley yanked off her bonnet, kicked off her slippers, and slid down the bank into the river.

The cold water reached for her hungrily, foaming about her as she waded waist-deep, doing its best to tug her off her feet. Directly in front of her Damon surfaced, gasping for air, his black hair plastered flat against his head. His dark eyes stared into hers for a moment before he went under again.

Had Freddie told her that a drowning man rose up only once? Or was it twice? Thrice? She could not remember. Ashley plunged beneath the surface, groping ahead of her, fighting the current as she searched for the man called Damon, afraid she might already be too late to save him. She stayed under until she was desperate for breath.

As her head broke the surface, something gripped her shoulder, startling her into swallowing water. Choking and coughing, she gazed in surprise at the dark-haired man whose hand was on her shoulder. Before she had a chance to collect herself, he grabbed her around the waist and began pulling her toward shore.

"Don't panic," he told her. "I shall save you."

Indignant, Ashley fought to free herself. "I can swim," she informed him.

Instead of releasing her, he grasped her all the more tightly. Moments later, her flailing feet touched bottom. "Let me go!" she cried, as she fought for stable footing.

He ceased pulling her toward the riverbank but did not obey her command. Standing facing her, he drew her closer, pressing her body to his, her thighs to his thighs, her breasts to his chest. Bemused, she did not move while he bent his head and his lips found hers.

He was kissing her! In her shock at his effrontery, Ashley allowed more than an instant or two to pass before she tried to push him away. To no avail. Freddie's advice rang in her ears. "If 'n a bloke grabs ye unawares-like, Miss, 'ook 'im round the back of 'is ankle with yer foot 'n' sorta jerk. Makes 'im topple 'n' ye'll go free."

Ashley tried it. Damon lost his balance in a most satisfactory manner, but unfortunately did not let her go; consequently they both went under. Squirming away from him, she rose and made for the bank, scrambling up its slippery, muddy surface with all the dignity she could manage. Which was not very much. She did not deign to look behind her at the man who had tricked her into believing he was drowning, then added insult to injury by kissing her.

The blond man evidently had followed their progress downstream, because he stood waiting on the path with her slippers and bonnet in his hand.

"Thank you," she murmured, as she reached first for her shoes, then her bonnet.

"Liam Gounod, at your service, Miss," he said, with an exaggerated bow that almost tipped him over.

She had slid her muddy feet into her shoes and was starting to place the bonnet over her soggy hair when a deep voice said from behind her, "Fascinating fish in this river. What do you think of the one I caught, Liam?"

Ashley whirled to face Damon, dropping her bonnet in the process. With dismay she watched it bounce off the top of the riverbank and tumble down into the water. Turning back to Damon, she glared at him, adding another misdemeanor to his list of transgressions.

His gaze did not cross hers; he was not even looking at her face. Instead, he appeared to be examining the rest of her with an unsettling intentness. The gleam in his eyes made her belatedly realize that the mud smeared on her gown from the bank did little to hide how revealingly its wet folds clung to her body. Embarrassed and angry, she flushed, the loss of her bonnet forgotten.

Damon sketched a bow. "I have never seen you look more charming, Miss Blayne."

What in high heaven was he talking about? Ashley did not intend to linger long enough to unravel the puzzle; she wished only to quit his company as soon as possible. "That is not my name," she said dismissively, turning away. "If you will excuse me . . ."

His hand clamped down on her arm. "I beg to differ," he said. "Your disguise has failed, Alcida. Even Lincolnshire mud cannot hide your charms from your admirers. As you may or may not know, I am one of them."

"I say," Liam put in. "It *is* Alcida Blayne. Clever of you to recognize her. Didn't have a clue, m'self."

"Please release me." With considerable effort Ashley kept her voice from quivering. Mrs. Graham's warning about high-flyers was all too true. Whatever game they were playing unnerved her, but she knew better than to show her unease. One of the minister's quotes came to her mind, not from the Bible, as was his usual practice, but from Shakespeare:

> *Cowards die many times before their deaths;*
> *The valiant never taste of death but once.*

That being true, she told herself, I refuse to be afraid of these London fops. I am in the right; they are in the wrong.

Donning her frostiest expression, she pulled free of Damon and crossed her arms over her breasts. Then she deliberately looked him up and down, noticing for the first time what a sorry sight he was with his fashionable clothes as sodden and muddy as her gown.

"Was it not enough that you stole a boat, lost the oars, and overturned it?" she asked. "Must you also detain a lady against her will?"

"What gambit is this?" Damon demanded. "I am not a thief; I assumed the boat was beached for all to use. As for you being a lady, under the circumstances I shan't question your application of the word." His tone left little doubt in her mind that he did not consider her a lady.

"Heard you sing jus' last month," Liam said to her, before she could express her indignation. "Sweet 's a wee yellow bird from the Isles, 's what I told Lord Damon here."

Ashley glanced at him in confusion, understanding nothing Liam had said except the "Lord Damon." A lord, was he? She raised her chin. His title was no excuse for his behavior. Whether the kiss came from a lout or a lord, she *was* a lady, and not to be touched against her will.

"Much drinking, little thinking," she muttered, quoting Mrs. Graham.

"The lady must be referring to you," Lord Damon informed Liam, who grinned sheepishly.

"At least he behaves like a gentleman," she snapped.

Lord Damon slanted her a wicked smile. "Ah, but Liam is content to be a worshipper from afar. I hope to come closer. Much closer. I have heard canaries make delightful pets."

What was this nonsense about the little yellow birds called canaries? And why did they persist in calling

her "Miss Blayne"? Still, what did it matter? It was
nothing but a humbug to them. As for her, it was past
time to leave. She should have done so long before
this.

"I must go," she said, turning and walking briskly
away, her slippers squishing most unpleasantly because of her wet stockings.

"See you in London, Miss Blayne," Liam called
after her.

She made no acknowledgment to his nonsense.
Though Lord Damon remained silent, she half expected him to come striding after her. When he did
not, she assured herself she was relieved, refusing to
admit the feeling was more akin to disappointment.

Ashley did not turn to look around when she heard
the clop and rattle of a conveyance somewhere behind her. No doubt the squire had sent someone to
fetch his two houseguests. Her sodden skirt flopping
dismally around her ankles, she hurried on, wondering how she could explain her wet gown and whether
or not she should mention the missing boat. If she
told the entire story, Mrs. Graham was certain to be
shocked into resorting to her smelling salts.

When she was a young child in the Methodist orphanage, the Millses had taught her, as they taught
all their charges, to always be truthful. Since then,
experience had taught her that to tell the exact truth
every time led to more punishments than rewards.
While not a liar, Ashley had learned life ran smoother
for her if she left out parts of the truth and, on occasion, shaded it a trifle.

Perhaps it would be best not to mention the boat.
Telling Mr. Graham what had happened to it would

not lead to the boat's recovery but would reveal her encounter with the London high-flyers, upsetting both Grahams. The shocking state of her clothes could be explained away as the result of accidentally falling into Dane's Run. Mrs. Graham would then merely scold her for carelessness.

When she reached the stream inlet where the boat had been kept beached, she found Freddie waiting for her.

"Rats and mice!" he exclaimed, as soon as he saw her. "What befell ye? Where's yer straw bonnet, 'n' where's Master's boat?"

Not until then did she remember that, like the boat and oars, her bonnet was lost in the river. Understanding that Freddie would not be there without a reason, she dismissed the lost bonnet from her mind, and instead of replying to his questions, asked, "Why did you come to meet me?"

" 'Go find Miss Ashley,' Missus tells me. Sent 'is footman with a note, 'Is Grace did. Elsie in the kitchen, she told me Missus 'n' Master, they 'ad their 'eads together for ever so long afore they give the footman a note to take back. Musta been about ye."

Ashley stared at Freddie in confusion. Was he speaking of the Duke of Roxton? She'd seen the duke in the village several times, a dark and dour man, neither young nor old, a man everyone seemed to be wary of. He was a widower who lived at Humber's Harp, an ancient and gloomy old stone mansion north of Louth. He did not mingle with the local gentry nor welcome London visitors to his home. Had not there also been whispers about a pact with the devil? What could he possibly want with her?

Shaking her head, she said, "The note could not have anything to do with me."

"Then why did Missus order me to find ye?" Freddie demanded.

She could not deny Freddie's logic. At the same time she recalled that the last time she had encountered the duke in Louth, he had fixed his gaze on her for longer than she had liked, making her skin crawl. She had longed to turn away but had been unable to. Ashley swallowed. An hour earlier her prickling thumbs had warned her of a change, but she did not want to believe it involved the Duke of Roxton.

A damp breeze blew off the river, chilling Ashley and making her shiver in her wet clothes, temporarily driving everything else from her mind. She could almost hear Mrs. Graham's scolding voice, ordering her to hurry and change before she caught her death of cold.

"I had best get home," she said.

Freddie nodded in agreement and fell into step behind her on the path from the stream to the house. "Soaked to the bone, ye be," he told her. " 'Ow come ye fell in the Run, light-foot like ye be?"

She couldn't tell Freddie what had happened because he would tell Elsie and soon everyone would know. "The mud along the bank is slippery," she said. The truth, if not all of it.

Ashley smiled to herself, remembering that Lord Damon must be as uncomfortably wet as she. He well deserved such a fate. How dared he kiss her! Her fingers touched her lips as though to feel for a remnant of that kiss. When she realized what she was doing, she snatched her hand away and hurried her pace. She refused to waste her time dwelling on Lord Damon and his despicable behavior.

" 'E's got a daughter," Freddie said, from behind her.

"Lord Damon?" she was surprised into asking.

"Lord Damon? The London toff 'oo's got an old aunt at Lancaster 'All? What a pair o' 'igh-stepping blacks 'e drives."

Lancaster Hall? Then he was not one of Squire Mitred's guests. "I know nothing of Lord Damon," she said.

"Said 'is name, ye did. 'E don't 'ave no daughter, 'e ain't married, neither. Meant 'Is Grace, I did."

Ashley nodded; she had heard about a child. How dreary it must be for a young girl in that gloomy gray mansion. Was she, like Rapunzel, kept locked in the ugly old tower? "I don't want to think about Humber's Harp," she muttered. Nor did she want to dwell on the duke, even less on his note to the Grahams that might be about her.

"Don't 'ave nothing to do with that wicked stone pile nor 'im what lives there," Freddie advised.

God knew she did not want to. "My life is going to change," she told Freddie. "I pray it will be for the better." But recalling the way the duke had stared at her that time in Louth brought a shiver that had nothing to do with her wet clothes.

She hugged herself, suddenly apprehensive that the change might not be one she cared for—might, in fact, be worse than she could imagine.

Two

To Ashley's surprise, Mrs. Graham dismissed her damp and disheveled condition with no more than a disapproving sniff, saying, "Change your clothes and set yourself to rights and do so quickly. We are expecting a visit from the Reverend Mr. Mills, a meeting at which I have convinced Mr. Graham you should be present."

Elsie, the maid-of-all-work, brought hot water upstairs from the kitchen so Ashley could wash.

"Took some mud bath, ye did, Miss," Elsie observed, as she helped Ashley off with the wet and soiled gown. "Never thought I'd see the day ye fell in Dane's Run. Likely ye'll come clean with scrubbing. Not yer gown. 'Tis spoilt forever and aye."

Ashley sighed in agreement. Shedding her undergarments and stockings, she climbed into the tin tub and eased down into several inches of tepid water.

"Want me to wash yer hair?" Elsie asked. "Brought up some of Missus' camphor and borax mix, I did."

"I would appreciate your help, Elsie. Mrs. Graham asked me to hurry."

"Master sent Ernst off to fetch the minister," Elsie commented, as she rubbed the mixture into Ashley's hair. "Cook says on account of the note from His

Grace. Minister's the right one to deal with the devil, Cook says."

Ashley, wrinkling her nose as the odor of camphor permeated her bedchamber, paused in her ablutions to say, "The Duke of Roxton is not the devil, Elsie," wondering while she spoke if she was trying to convince the maid or herself.

"Maybe not, Miss, but there's them what swear Old Scratch ain't no stranger at Humber's Harp. Wouldn't work there if they was to give me a golden guinea for every pail of water I lugged, that I wouldn't."

Elsie's words burned in Ashley's mind while the maid rinsed her hair. Didn't Mrs. Graham always warn that where there was smoke, there was fire? That gossip, while evil in itself, often contained more than a grain of truth?

She had no doubt that because Mr. Graham had consented to her presence at the meeting with the minister, the Duke of Roxton's note must concern her. "I can't think what the duke might want with me," she blurted.

"I can," Elsie said darkly. When Ashley glanced up at her inquiringly, the maid shook her head. "Blabbed too much already, I did. Ma always scolded me for not keeping me mummer dubbed."

Ashley could not pry another word out of her. By the time she had dried off and was dressed in her second best gown, she was such a bundle of nerves that her fingers shook as she pinned her damp, rebellious curls into the intricate French knot Mrs. Mills had taught her.

"When I was a girl my mother had a French maid,"

the minister's wife had explained. "Say what you will about the French, much of it deserved—they do have a certain flair when it comes to fashion."

At least this gown, cut down from one of Mrs. Graham's voluminous, invariably dark green dresses, boasted a more fashionable waistline, though the neck remained high. Mrs. Graham did not believe in young ladies revealing their bosoms to all and sundry any more than she approved of what she termed "frivolous curls," a rather accurate description of Ashley's auburn hair if it was not kept strictly confined.

Elsie, draining water from the tub into a slop pail, looked up at her, asking, "Ain't that the minister's rig I hear?"

Ashley nodded. Taking a deep breath, she took one last glance around the room as if looking for an escape. There was no escape, she knew that, and the delay did more harm than good, for Elsie's expression mirrored her own apprehension, thus increasing hers. She reminded herself that not knowing what lay ahead could be more frightening than discovering exactly what one must face, and walked determinedly from the room.

The green gown's cotton twill skirt rubbed stiffly against her ankles as she hesitantly descended the stairs.

Mrs. Graham was showing the minister to a seat in the front parlor, the roundabout upholstered in green striped damask, the corner chair reserved for important visitors.

"There you are," she said, when she caught sight of Ashley. "Don't, I pray, dawdle in the entry."

"Come in, come in, girl," Mr. Graham ordered gruffly.

"I trust this day finds you in good health," Mr. Mills said to her.

Ashley managed an affirmative, though she was not any too certain a dunking in Dane's Run was particularly salubrious.

Once all were seated, Ashley perched on the very edge of the most uncomfortable straight-backed chair in the parlor, the minister put a hand on each knee and gazed at Mr. Graham. "Perhaps you will be good enough to begin with an explanation. The message you sent by Ernst did not specify why I was to come here as soon as possible."

Always a man of few words, Mr. Graham nodded toward Ashley. "Concerns her. Need your advice."

"Does it have something to do with the Duke of Roxton?" the minister asked. "As you know, I abhor gossip, but since every man, woman, and child seemed to be discussing the event, I could not avoid hearing that His Grace's footman stopped here to deliver a note."

"Seems His Grace needs a governess for his daughter." Again Mr. Graham nodded toward Ashley. "Wants her."

"He offers a more than adequate stipend," Mrs. Graham put in. "But she will have to live at Humber's Harp." She began to gnaw on a knuckle, something Ashley had never seen her do. This obvious evidence of agitation added to Ashley's growing unease.

"I don't know, Mr. Mills," Mrs. Graham went on, "I simply do not know what answer we should give.

The note we sent back with the footman said no more than that we must consult you before replying."

Shooting Ashley a swift glance, the minister steepled his hands, and turning to Mrs. Graham, asked, "She has not accepted Mr. Laughlin's offer of marriage?"

Ashley cleared her throat. "No, sir," she said, before anyone else could speak, amazed that the words could get past the tightness in her throat. In the past Mrs. Mills had mentioned the possibility of Ashley's applying for a position as a governess, but there had never been an opening in the neighborhood and Mrs. Graham would not hear of her traveling to a city that rivaled Sodom and Gomorrah for wickedness, meaning London.

But governess to the Duke of Roxton's daughter? From nowhere the child's name came to her— Clematis, or so she had heard. The girl's name was of no matter; what concerned her was the possibility she might have to live at Humber's Harp—frightening to contemplate. Especially since there was no duchess in residence, His Grace's wife having died in an accident a few years before.

"Did you not care for Mr. Laughlin?" Mr. Mills persisted. "He is a respectable widower with the largest farm in the district."

"I refused Mr. Laughlin, and I have not changed my mind." Not for any number of guineas would she be persuaded to reveal her reasons. She might have been willing to try to mother his seven small children, but she would not have been able to bear him as a husband. His unsightly corpulence was bad enough, but the fact that he never seemed to bathe put him beyond the pale. In a word, his sour stench turned her stomach. She did not understand why the minister and the Grahams behaved as though they were not aware of how foul he smelled.

"How I see it, the girl just plain don't want to marry," Mr. Graham said.

"She is that particular," Mrs. Graham agreed. "Six offers for her, and not a one would she so much as consider."

"Despite your always excellent advice?" the minister asked.

Mrs. Graham gave a ladylike snort. "You must be aware that Ashley is not a tractable girl. As you know, we have done our best for her. I believe she is grateful, but it does not make her amenable to my advice."

"You and Mr. Graham have always been good to me," Ashley cried, upset by being talked about as though she were not present. "I am not unduly stubborn, truly. Nor am I a care-for-nobody. If the right man had offered for me. . . ." Her words trailed off as, unbidden, Lord Damon's face appeared before her, his dark hair dripping and a wicked glint in his eye.

Never, she told herself indignantly. Never would I conceive an interest in a rag-mannered, shockingly forward rake such as he is, much less marry him!

Not that he would ever ask for her hand. Lords did not marry country maidens, orphans with no family and no expectations.

"I take it the right man, whoever he may be, has not yet put in an appearance," the minister said, finally speaking directly to her, a slight edge to his voice.

Ashley reddened guiltily, Lord Damon still on her mind. "No, sir, I regret that he has not."

"You must realize that the Grahams cannot go on keeping you forever."

"I do understand they cannot," Ashley admitted.

The minister patted his steepled fingers together. "Accurate though it sometimes proves to be, I never judge man or woman on the basis of common gossip. His Grace, of course, attends a church other than ours. I shall consult with his minister and if he, being better acquainted with the duke than we are, assures me Ashley will be safe within the portals of Humber's Harp, then I will be able to see it clear to advise her to accept the position. Because of the good offices of my wife, she has been well trained in deportment, language, arithmetic, history, and geography and should be capable of transmitting her knowledge to a child."

"Girl's bright enough, granted," Mr. Graham said. "Too bright, sometimes, to suit me. Or any man, likely enough. May be better for all concerned she goes for a governess rather than a wife. Should do all right with the duke's daughter. Remember His Grace as a boy riding over the countryside. Had a good seat even then. Never believed that ta-ra-diddle about him and the devil, myself. Fools prattling."

"We shall await your advice," Mrs. Graham told the minister.

No one has asked me what I wish to do, Ashley thought, aware that they believed there was no reason to. Since she would not marry any who had offered for her, she must find a way to support herself. The

Grahams had been good to her but she was, after all, not their daughter; she was a fosterling.

It wasn't the idea of becoming a governess that frightened her; what she feared to do was go to live at Humber's Harp. In the same house as the Duke of Roxton.

As far as Ashley was concerned, the remainder of the day passed without her being a part of it. In a daze, she bade a polite goodbye to the minister before helping Mrs. Graham with the household chores.

Only later, when she handed out a pail of peelings and parings for Freddie to take for the pigs' trough, did he gaze at her with such a stricken expression that she was jolted from her trance.

"Ain't likely any of us'll ever seen ye again," he said mournfully.

"Nothing is settled," she assured him.

" 'Twill be. What 'Is Grace wants, 'e gets."

"Even if I do go, I shall come back for a visit now and again."

"Ye won't."

Ashley felt like shaking him. Did not he understand his gloomy predictions made her feel worse? "Freddie, no matter what happens, 'twill not be the end of the world." Her exasperation showed in her voice.

" 'Twill for ye. Better ye go to London 'n' be that lord's bit o' muslin than be the prey o' the devil."

Ashley could not believe her ears. "What lord?"

"Ye called 'im by name—Lord Damon. Ernst heard a couple 'o London gents took Master's boat, so I figure you must o' run across 'em on the riverbank 'n' that's how come ye fell in."

"I jumped in," she said resignedly, no longer caring if he did tell Elsie. "I thought he was drowning and I meant to save him."

"Lord Damon?" Freddie shook his head. "I seen 'im swimming more 'n' once in the Run. Champion, 'e is."

"I know that. Now. He deliberately played a May game with me."

Freddie shook his head. " 'Ave to get up early to 'oax ye, 'e would."

"Well, he did. And just what did you mean by a bit o' muslin?"

Freddie's round and freckled face turned bright red. "Ain't gonna tell Missus, be ye?"

"No, I just want to know what the phrase means." Actually she had a fair idea. This might be the country, not London, but men were men and ladies had best beware.

"A fancy lady, like," he muttered.

"And that is what you are advising me to do? Become Lord Damon's fancy lady?" Her outrage showed in her voice.

"Don't get on yer 'igh horse, Miss. Didn't mean no 'arm. Figured 'e'd treat ye right 'n' all, 'stead o' serving ye up to the devil on a silver platter, like the other's gonna do."

"No one is going to serve me to the devil on *any* kind of a platter," she said firmly. "Neither do I intend to become any man's bit o' muslin. Especially Lord Damon's."

Freddie never stayed crushed for long. "What ye

got against 'im? Lord Damon's a right one, 'e is. What they call top-o'-the-trees in London.''

"I don't care whether he is at the top or down among the roots with the worms. I am *not* interested in Lord Damon. Or in discussing him any further.'' Ashley frowned at Freddie's suddenly sly look, turned on her heel, and went back into the house.

That was what she got for being, as Mrs. Graham put it, "too familiar" with the servants. As a rule, Freddie's indomitable spirit as well as the fact he, too, was an orphan spoke to something within her, but this evening he had come far too close to outright impudence. Lord Damon's bit o' muslin, indeed!

The idea of anyone believing she could ever stoop to becoming a fancy lady was shocking enough— whatever was the matter with Freddie? And then he had dared to add Lord Damon's name, fueling the flames of her indignation.

To make matters worse, Lord Damon had treated her as though he assumed she *was* one of those loose creatures. Her brow furrowed. Why had he and his friend insisted she was "Miss Blayne"? They could hardly have planned such a hum in advance, for they had no reason to think they would meet a young lady on the path. And Liam Gounod had seemed far too ripe to be alert enough to participate in a scheme-of-the-moment to flummox her.

Was it possible there actually *was* an Alcida Blayne in London? But if so, what could have been their purpose in pretending *she* was Miss Blayne? With insufficient clues, the puzzle was beyond her ability to solve.

"Do stop wool-gathering," Mrs. Graham admonished. "Have you forgotten tomorrow is washday and Hannah will arrive before six? If you don't come and help me with the sorting, we shall never get the clothes ready for her to wash in the morning."

As she obeyed, Ashley wished, not for the first time, that she and Mrs. Graham were as close as mother and daughter. If they had been, she could pour out her fears and apprehensions. But though the Grahams had taken her in and taken care of her, they had never treated her quite the way they would have treated a daughter of their own.

Not like her own mother would have treated her. Whoever and wherever her real mother might be. Since she refused to believe her mother had died bearing her, Ashley clung to the idea that there must have been a compelling reason forcing her mother to abandon her. A reason that so far had prevented her mother's return to claim her. If only. . . .

She was jolted from her fantasy by Mr. Graham stomping into the back room, exclaiming, "My boat's gone missing. Had enough of those high-and-mighty Londoners and their smoky behavior. I'm off to Squire Mitred's."

"Now, Mr. Graham," Mrs. Graham said placatingly. "Squire won't want to be bothered what with visitors there and all."

Mr. Graham shook his fist in the air. "His nimby-brained visitors stole my boat!"

"No, they did not." Ashley spoke without thinking, forcing her to scramble to come up with a partial truth in order to avoid revealing what really had happened. "Freddie heard Lady Lancaster's nephew had borrowed the boat."

Mr. Graham scowled at her. "You might have told me."

"I intended to, sir," she said.

"Borrowed," he muttered. "Humph!"

"If Lady Lancaster hears of it," Mrs. Graham put in, "she will have the boat returned to us."

All three of them understood that the lady would hear soon enough. Spread by the servants and tradespeople, gossip traveled rapidly through the countryside.

"Why can't they keep their sap-skull pranks confined to the city?" Mr. Graham demanded. "Bothering honest hardworking farmers is nothing to be proud of."

Ashley was in full agreement with this sentiment, but when Mr. Graham went on to say he would not set foot in London to save his life, she thought his stand far too extreme. London, as she imagined the city, must be a fascinating place, a place she longed to visit.

Mrs. Mills had been to Vauxhall Gardens before she married. "A fairyland," was how she described the wonders there. Ashley sighed. Instead of Vauxhall Gardens, the only sight she could look forward to seeing was Humber's Harp. Involuntarily, she shivered.

"I knew it," Mrs. Graham said. "I was certain you would take a chill from what happened to you during your ill-ventured walk along the river. Why Dane's Run holds such interest for you, I have no idea." She leaned over and felt Ashley's forehead. "Best take yourself directly up to bed while I prepare a tisane.

An ounce of prevention is worth a pound of cure, as I always say."

Though she had little stomach for Mrs. Graham's ill-tasting potions, Ashley knew better than to protest. If she pretended to agree, she might find a way to dispose of the tisane without swallowing it. While if she argued, Mrs. Graham was sure to stand over her to make certain she took every last drop of the evil mixture.

She was in luck, for Elsie brought up the medicine along with a hot brick to tuck into the bed for her feet. As soon as the maid left, the tisane went directly into the slop jar inside the commode stand. Already in her nightgown, Ashley slid under the covers. Unused to being in bed before full darkness, she propped her head up on her two pillows and gazed out the window at the gathering dusk.

In the evening sky, one bright star twinkled between the horns of a sickle moon. Mrs. Mills had taught her how to recognize some of the constellations in the heavens and she had learned enough to know this one bright star was not connected to her favorite constellation, the Pleiades, the Seven Sisters. As a child in the orphanage she had sometimes pretended she was one of seven sisters, a part of a large, loving family.

The myth about the Pleiades was both sad and beautiful. Relentlessly pursued by Orion, the sisters begged the father of the gods for help and were changed into doves so they could fly up and hide among the stars.

If only I really did have six sisters, Ashley thought wistfully. Or even one sister. How wonderful it must

be to grow up sharing with someone who was a blood
relation, someone who would always be there if
needed.

But she had no sisters. Nor was any ancient deity
likely to heed her plea and change her into a dove
so she could fly up among the stars. There was only
the Grahams and Mr. Mills. If the minister so advised
them, and she suspected he would, her path could
only lead directly to Humber's Harp and whatever
dark and dire fate awaited her there.

Three

Long before they reached the Dower House, the only building remaining intact after Lancaster Hall's disastrous fire of '06, Charles Jordon, Marquess of Damon, had decided the better part of valor would be to pretend he had fallen into the river. The grizzled groom driving the ancient landau pulled by two equally ancient nags could be counted on to blab about his sopping clothes, so the matter could not be smoothed over without some explanation. He dared not lay the truth on the carpet for Aunt Talissa to wax indignant over. Fond as he was of the old gal, he was in no condition to listen to one of her famous lectures.

Neither he nor Liam was a four-bottle man, but to own the truth, they had rather overindulged at the Harp and Whistle in Louth. If he had not been ever so slightly foxed he would never have appropriated the boat to begin with, much less dropped the oars overboard and then tipped the blasted crate over for good measure. Cold river water was the devil's own cure for unripening a man shockingly fast.

On the other hand, Liam, slumped against him snoring, was still out for the count. With luck Liam would not recall much of the day's doings and would therefore not indulge his fatal tendency to talk too much. Likely enough he would not even remember their odd encounter with Alcida Blayne.

According to London tittle-tattle, the lovely Miss Blayne had not yet chosen a protector. The latest *on-dit* favored a German prince Damon had yet to meet and did not particularly care to become acquainted with. Perhaps the lady had found the prince as odious as Damon suspected him of being and she had flown away to avoid an undesirable entanglement. She certainly had been in masquerade, posing as the very essence of a country miss. If he had not recognized her, she would have gammoned him the way she had Liam.

Despite the discomfort of wet clothes and Liam's not inconsiderable bulk leaning on him, Damon smiled. He would be willing to wager considerably more than a groat that he had been one of the few men who could boast he had kissed the fair Alcida. For all her on-stage smiles and professional charm, he had been told by more than one dashing blade that she could be as prickly as a hedgehog if a man tried to get too close.

To his way of thinking, a kiss was like a toe in the door—the passage was no longer completely barred. Here in the wilds of Lincolnshire, he had the delightful Miss Blayne all to himself and he intended to take full advantage of his good fortune. Ignoring his present discomfort while anticipating later pleasure, he spent the rest of the ride to Lancaster Hall planning his first move.

"A milliner," he exclaimed, as the carriage pulled up in front of the Dower House.

Liam jerked awake, sat up and glanced around in confusion. "What?" he asked. "Where?"

"Not to worry, old man," Damon drawled. "You can sleep it off in one of Aunt Tally's guest rooms."

He helped Liam from the landau, handed him over to Langdon, the butler, at the front door and went in search of his aunt.

"*You* fell into Dane's Run?" Lady Lancaster asked incredulously a few minutes later in the morning room. "Nonsense."

"Muddy banks," Damon added hastily. "Liam and I were having a bit of fun and I slipped."

She eyed him with raised eyebrows. "You have never been successful at fabrication. At least not with me."

Damon understood he would have to reveal at least a portion of the truth. "Actually there was a local boat involved. Unfortunately, I tipped it over."

"I knew there was more. Whose boat?"

Damon shrugged.

She sighed. "I shall endeavor to discover the owner and you will see that either the boat is returned to him or that he receives ample compensation should it be irretrievably lost. For the moment I shall be satisfied by you marching straight up to your usual room and ridding yourself of those disgustingly wet and filthy clothes. Hot water will be forthcoming. Once you have made yourself decent, you may greet me properly and we shall discuss this further."

"Liam's with me. I told Langdon to find him a room. I trust you don't mind, Aunt Tally."

"You know young Gounod is welcome here as are

any of your friends." She made shooing motions with her hands. "Go!"

Louth was a far cry from London, Damon told himself as he climbed the broad staircase to his bedchamber. The village would have nothing to compare to Bond Street, but surely there must be a milliner somewhere in the area capable of constructing an acceptable bonnet. The hat would have to fit into Alcida Blayne's masquerade, so perhaps 'twas as well he would be dealing with a country milliner. 'Twould never do to present her with the latest fashion in London headgear.

Not if his plan was to be a success.

Damon woke to grayish light the next morning and found Liam Gounod at his windows, flinging open the curtains.

"A glorious morn," Liam exclaimed, as soon as Damon opened his eyes. "What say you to a brisk ride while we watch the sun come up?"

Damon groaned, sat up, looked out at a predawn sky, and muttered, "I felt sure after the ale we imbibed yesterday, you would be abed until noon. As for me, I prefer the sun to be *up* before I rise."

Liam grinned at him. "Country air revives me wonderfully." He ran his hands through his hair, disordering it more than a night's sleep had. "Not a trace of a head and I'm ravenous."

The previous day, while Liam had slept off the drink, Damon had managed to pay a visit to a local milliner and was to pick up the bonnet this morning. Liam had no place in his plan to ferret out the whereabouts of the delectable Alcida but he had not worked through how to prevent his friend from coming along.

"Might have imagined it." Liam frowned as he spoke. "Admit I was rather deep in my cups."

"Imagined what?" Damon feared the worst. If Liam recollected yesterday's happenings in any detail, he'd never be able to shake him.

"Unlikely, I realize, but I seem to recall you fell out of a boat."

Relieved, Damon swung his legs over the edge of the bed, stood and clapped a hand on his friend's shoulder. "Delighted to hear your memory is intact. The problem is, the boat was not mine. Aunt Tally has taken me to task about the episode, and I need your help."

"Always ready to aid a friend. You can count on me."

"I knew I could," Damon said, feeling some slight guilt. Yet didn't rules go by the board when fair cyprians were involved? "We must find that boat or I shall be forever in my aunt's bad graces."

Liam nodded. "Went down Dane's Run without you aboard, I take it."

"Bottom up. What I propose is this. You take one side of the river and I shall take the other. 'Twill do little good merely to search for the craft, we must ask those who live along the banks if they have spotted the boat or, perchance, hauled it out, believing it was abandoned. Do you recall the color?"

Liam's brow furrowed. "Dark green?" he hazarded.

Damon nodded. "With a flat bottom. Difficult boat

to turn over, but somehow I managed, thanks to the Harp and Whistle's potent country ale. A couple of oars were involved in the disaster, but I doubt we will recover those."

"Unlikely," Liam agreed. "I shall be ready to begin as soon as I break my fast. I vow I could devour a stag, horns and all."

"Aunt Tally's cook is unusually even-tempered, the odds are she'll not fuss unduly about two hungry men invading her domain."

The sun was halfway up the sky by the time Damon saw Liam across the horse and footbridge crossing Dane's Run near Lancaster Hall. "No need to go as far as where the Run empties into the Humber," he told Liam. "Five miles downriver or thereabouts is all the farther I plan to search."

Once the trees hid his friend from sight, Damon wheeled his bay and trotted up a rutted lane to the milliner's cottage, telling himself all was fair when it came to planning the acquisition of a new mistress, especially when she happened to be one of the most sought-after stage performers in all of London. If Liam discovered his ploy, he was sure his friend would not only understand but would forgive him as well.

Later, riding upriver toward Mitred Bridge, where that blasted boat had dumped him into the water, Damon was not as sanguine about his chances of finding Miss Blayne's hideaway. Despite discreet questioning in the area by a stableboy of Aunt Tally's that he given a shilling to, none of the locals had admitted there was a young lady from London staying nearby and amusing herself by dressing as a country maiden. His only choice was to return to the scene of the

accident and hope she would choose to walk by the
bridge again today.

Ashley hurried along the bank of Dane's Run, trying not to hear Freddie's parting words echoing in
her mind.

"Gonna meet Lord Damon again, be ye? Don't forget what I told ye."

She had done her best to ignore Freddie, but that
was an impossibility.

"Yonnie, the 'ostler over to the Inn," Freddie had
gone on, " 'e vows 'tis better to be a fancy lady than
a wife. Ye get jewels 'n' clothes 'n' 'e takes ye all over
London while 'is wife, if 'e's got one, sits home doing
'er 'broidery."

"I am *not* meeting Lord Damon," she had snapped.

Which, whether Freddie believed her or not, was
no more than the truth. When Mrs. Graham had un-
expectedly presented her with the entire day off, to
do with as she liked, Ashley could hardly wait to reach
her secret spot in the glen. There, in the hush among
the trees, with only the splash of the streamlet trick-
ling into the hidden pool, perhaps she could calm
her mind enough so she would be able to face the
inevitable with equanimity.

Because, though the minister had not yet returned
to speak to the Grahams, her fate seemed sealed. She
would become young Lady Clematis's governess, she
would reside at Humber's Harp and she would have
to deal with the duke as best she could. If only she
had a female confidante to discuss the matter with.
Mrs. Mills might have been a possibility, but she had

been ill recently with a heart affliction and Ashley did not wish to upset her in any way.

As she neared Mitred Bridge, her recollection of the previous day's contretemps banished her gloom. How henwitted she had been to allow Lord Damon to kiss her! She should have known better than to leap into the river to save him in the first place. Since she knew all the boys in the neighborhood could swim, she should have realized it followed that most men must be able to. Liam Gounod must be an exception—but then, it had not been him she had tried to rescue. *He* would never had tried to kiss her, she was sure.

Why in high heaven couldn't she dismiss the stolen kiss Lord Damon had taken from her? It was over and done with, after all, and chances were they would never meet again. If she knew what had occurred, Mrs. Graham would certainly remind her that she should be grateful worse had not followed the kiss.

As Ashley set foot on the bridge, she thought she heard a horse snort. Pausing, she glanced around but saw neither horse nor rider, and though she waited for several minutes, no one came into view. Satisfied that her secret was safe, she hurried across the bridge and plunged into a thicket, following an almost invisible path that led past a marsh where scraps of netting over the ditches fluttered in the breeze, bringing her attention to the remnants of a duck pipe decoy near a drying-up pond.

Ashley's steps slowed while she gazed at the trap, one that gave the birds no chance at all to escape. Shaking her head, she passed by and soon the path led into a copse where once-pollarded trees grew tall and thick. Squire Mitred owned much of the land by this section of Dane's Run, but the grove of trees, she'd discovered by careful questioning, belonged to Lady Lancaster. So, of course, she was trespassing, but since she was no poacher, she did not believe anyone would care.

To avoid discovery, Damon had abandoned his bay, tying it to a stout sapling in a thicket near the riverbank. Now on foot, temporarily lurking behind the dubious cover of a patch of reeds, he watched his quarry disappear into the gloom underneath the old trees in what Aunt Tally called Viking Woods. The tiny patch of forest was Lancaster land; he knew it well, having explored the woods as a boy.

Could she have found his hidden pool in the glen?

He frowned, feeling unaccountably put out that this London songbird should land in the wooded paradise he had as a lad regarded as his private place.

Stuff and nonsense, he admonished himself. He was no longer a stripling; he was a grown man. Furthermore, as a connoisseur of London songbirds, his interest lay in the lady herself rather than in the glen; and since he had tracked her to her watering place, success lay within his grasp. Holding the hatbox firmly by its cord, he slipped from the reeds and followed her into the trees.

Concealed behind a screen of branches, Ashley gazed at the pool with pleasure. Because of the trees' thick canopy, the water looked dark, but she knew it was really crystal clear. Seating herself on an old blanket she'd cached here a year ago, Ashley flung off her bonnet, removed her slippers, then rolled down her stockings and slipped them off. Rising, she tested the water with one bare toe. Cold, yet not so frigid as in April. Lifting her skirts to her knees, she was preparing to wade in the shallows when an all-too-familiar voice froze her in place.

"I have come upon a neried, if I am not mistaken," Lord Damon said, from behind her. "A veritable water nymph. I consider myself doubly fortunate that my neried possesses delightful nether limbs rather than a fish's forked tail."

Ashley, her face flaming, dropped her skirts. Heart pounding, she turned to face him. "Sir," she said, as coolly as she could manage, "this is a private place."

"Quite so. The property of my aunt's, I believe."

His sudden appearance in the glen had addled her reasoning—how could she have forgotten he was Lady Lancaster's nephew? But she refused to be intimidated. "Have you come to run me off for trespassing?" she asked.

"Certainly not. Had I known you were coming here I would have brought along a picnic basket. As it is, all I can offer is this." Three steps put him close enough to try to hand her what was unmistakably a hatbox.

Rather than accepting the round box, she examined him. How different his appearance" was compared to when he had climbed from the river. She eyed his gray jacket, worn with a soft white scarf at the neck rather than the usual stiff cravat, and decided it must be the very latest in London fashion for country attire.

"The box is not mine," she told him, eyeing her

slippers sitting primly beside the blanket with her stockings folded across them. She must leave immediately, but she could hardly go barefooted. Obviously she could not replace her stockings in front of him, so she would have to slide her bare feet into the slippers.

"You are wrong about the box and its contents." He opened the lid. Inside, nestled among tissue paper, lay a straw hat with a wide brim, made to be held on the head with a twist of filmy green gauze. Tiny green silk ivy leaves twined about the base of the crown.

"The least I can do to make amends is to replace the bonnet you lost to the river. I apologize most humbly for being somewhat in my cups. Had I not been, I would have realized that your plunge into Dane's Run was a brave attempt to rescue me."

Since an apology was the last thing she had expected from him, Ashley found herself at a loss for words. "I did not know you could swim," she said finally.

Lord Damon set the hatbox onto her blanket. "I find it amazing that you apparently can swim. Most young ladies of my acquaintance are not so talented as you. In any way."

Ashley, who had begun to let down her guard, stiffened at his last few words, not certain of what he meant and not trusting his tone of voice. She should not remain here alone with him. It was neither proper nor prudent, and it might well not be safe.

"I refer to your musical talent, of course," he said hastily, evidently reading her expression.

Musical talent? Though it was true she often sang

at church fairs and occasionally at musical evenings arranged by friends of the Grahams, how would Lord Damon hear of this? Almost immediately she answered her own question. From Lady Lancaster, of course.

As if following her train of thought, he said, "I visited my aunt rather often when I was a boy, so I am quite familiar with the countryside. I confess I am pleased that you are the one who discovered my secret pool."

Ashley's eyes widened. "You have been to the glen before?"

"Not in years." He gazed around at the trees, up at the leafy canopy shading them from the sun and then focused on the pool. Still looking at the water, he smiled. "Few places remain as wonderful as one believed they were as a child. This is even lovelier than I remembered. A peaceful nook, hidden from those who might not appreciate its quiet beauty."

"Oh, yes, I do agree," she said eagerly. His words touched a chord within her, making her quite forget she should be fleeing rather than lingering, leading her to be inclined to think she had been too hasty in condemning Lord Damon. True, he'd misbehaved the day before, but had not he taken the trouble to explain and apologize?

If he had been deep enough in his cups, perhaps he did not even recall the kiss. For some reason she did not care to pursue this line of thought.

"Am I wrong in believing that my friend Liam Gounod told you my name?" he asked.

"Inadvertently, Lord Damon," she admitted.

He bent his head, sketching a bow. "At your service, Miss. . . ." He paused, looking perplexed. "Alas, I fear I cannot bring your name to mind. Do forgive me."

"Miss Ashley Douglas," she told him, relieved that he had no intention of continuing with the Alcida Blayne humbug.

He captured her hand before she realized what he intended, bringing it to his lips. For an electrifying moment his lips brushed against the back of her hand. "Delighted, Miss Douglas," he murmured.

There is nothing amiss, she assured herself. Nothing to give offense. 'Tis no more than a proper greeting.

"Will you think me too forward if I remove my boots and wade in the pool with you?" he asked.

Did she mind? Ashley considered. Perhaps she ought to be shocked at the mere suggestion but she was not. After all, this had been his pool before it was hers, and truth be known, the very pool itself belonged to his relative, not hers.

"I see no harm in it," she said primly, aware that she was being most daring. She should not even be alone with Lord Damon, much less contemplating going wading with him. But she wanted to so very much, and after all, who was to know?

He promptly sat down on her blanket and began tugging off his boots. Watching him disrobe even so slightly in front of her caused Ashley to avert her gaze. She turned toward the pool, feeling she had somehow gotten herself into a more intimate situation than she had meant to. Harmless though wading together had seemed at first blush, was anything harmless where Lord Damon was concerned? Had she taken her first step toward becoming a fancy lady? *His* fancy lady?

"Like a duck pipe decoy," she told herself. "Once lured in, there may be no way out."

He frowned up at her and then, barefooted, rose to face her. "To what, may I ask, are you referring?" he demanded.

Ashley flushed when she realized she had, without meaning to, spoken aloud. Gathering her wits, she sputtered, "I—I noticed the remnants of one of those decoys in the marsh."

"I saw the duck pipe. But I received the distinct impression you were comparing the decoy trap to something else."

"Oh, no! No, I . . ." She paused, searching desperately for an explanation that would not reveal what she had been thinking, finally grasping at a partial truth. "When I went past the trap I found myself distressed by the realization that the poor ducks, once lured into the net-covered ditches, have no escape. The hunter at the narrow end of the pipe grabs them one by one and wrings their necks. 'Tis not at all sporting."

Lord Damon's eyebrows rose. In disbelief, she decided, even though he merely said, "I agree that shooting ducks is the more sporting approach. Not every hunter with a gun has a perfect aim."

Still flustered, she eyed him from under her lashes, certain that whatever the circumstances, his aim would bring down his prey each and every time. And she greatly feared that at the moment, he might be hunting her.

Four

Damon wondered why Alcida—or Ashley, as she insisted on being called—appeared to be in a quake about wading with him in the pool. He had been careful not to insist that she *was* Alcida or that she was playing an undergame and she had seemed to accept his apparent change in attitude at face value. When he first proposed that they wade together she had hesitated, then rather formally agreed.

Her change in disposition occurred when he sat down to remove his boots. Surely the sight of his bare feet was not shocking enough to throw a London songbird into a fit of the vapors!

There *had* been her odd remark about it being like decoy pipes, "it" referring to what? She had refused to elucidate. He could not for the life of him see how permitting him to wade with her could have any relation to ducks being trapped and having their necks wrung.

But of course, ladies, whether their reputations were tarnished or spotless, often made nonsensical remarks. He would do well to ignore the matter and get on with his plan.

Eyeing her without obviously staring, so as not to rattle her further, he confirmed his opinion that winning Alcida would be worth any amount of effort. Though the unusually high neck of her excessively plain forest green gown concealed her breasts, the material clung to the curves of her unrevealed bosom in a most tantalizing fashion. She presently chose to look anywhere rather than at him, but he had already noticed how the gown deepened the green of her eyes, eyes holding secrets he longed to decipher.

Curls of auburn hair escaping from the restraining twist at the back of her head framed her oval face most charmingly, and the now fading blush enhanced her delicate coloring. In truth, she was a rare beauty.

Easy, he warned himself. She is no innocent filly to be lured to your hand by the offering of a sugar lump. Though she looked to be not a day over nineteen at the most, her time on the stage had surely taught her to be wary of offerings, no matter how tempting in appearance.

Deciding on his approach, he bowed deeply, held out his arm, and very formally inquired, "Would Miss Douglas do me the favor of granting me the first wade of the morning?"

She stared blankly at him for a long moment, then smiled, showing a beguiling dimple in her left cheek. "I shall be pleased to, Lord Damon," she replied. She placed one hand on his arm and caught up her skirt with the other.

Adhering to the pattern he had set, he led her slowly and solemnly to the pool, said, "Allow me to test the temperature," and dipped one foot into the water.

"Acceptable," he pronounced, eased her hand

from his arm until he could clasp it in his own, and drew her into the shallows of the pool with him. "May I say you wade most charmingly? This cannot be your first attempt."

"Thank you, 'tis not," she said primly. "Though always before, I waded alone."

"Do you not find, like the waltz, 'tis more agreeable with a companion?"

"I cannot compare the two, sir, since I have never waltzed."

If she insisted on playing the innocent maiden to the hilt, he was willing to oblige. "When the happy occasion occurs, I can only hope to be your first partner. Perhaps you will do me the honor at a country dance or mayhap in London. I trust the time will be soon."

Her sigh seemed to come from the bottom of her heart. "Alas, I fear there will never be such a time."

"Pray, do not say so, for you doom me to eternal misery."

"No," she murmured, so low he barely caught the words. "If anyone is doomed, I am." To his utmost surprise, she pulled free of his grasp, covered her face with her hands and burst into tears.

This waterfall of hers seemed to be genuine enough, for she continued to sob even after he had guided her from the pool and drawn her down onto the blanket. Feeling at a loss—how he disliked feminine tears—he put an arm around her. She leaned her head against his chest and cried as though her heart would break.

Few events left Damon at a loss, but this was one of them. "There, there," he murmured, feeling most ineffectual as he patted her back, wondering what could have set her off. True, she was an actress, but he believed her present emotion was genuine.

At last she eased away from him, produced a handkerchief from some hidden fold, and began dabbing at her eyes. "What must you think of me?" she said brokenly.

"Something untoward must have disturbed you deeply," he replied. "I trust I gave no offense."

Gazing at him, she blinked back new tears. Her voice shook when she spoke. "Not you. No, not you. I cannot begin to tell you—" She broke off, shaking her head. " 'Tis no trouble of yours, I shan't burden you with mine."

How lovely she was with her tear-bright eyes, flushed face, and quivering lips. He had to fight his impulse to gather her into his arms. Against his better judgment he said, "If I can help you in any way, I shall be glad to."

"No one can help me." He watched her teeth nibble at her luscious lower lip and was undone.

Cupping her face in his hands, he kissed her, gently at first, then, when she didn't push him away, more urgently, coaxing a response.

Ashley leaned into Lord Damon's kiss, at first merely wanting more of his comforting warmth, then feeling the sweet pressure of his lips unleash a thrilling need within her, one that demanded more than a brief kiss. Without realizing what she did, she lifted her arms, wrapping them around his shoulders to hold him to her so the kiss might be prolonged.

Before she understood what was happening, he'd gathered her close, teased her lips apart with his, and begun to caress her mouth with the tip of his tongue. Tremors of delight ran through her body, causing a moan of pleasure to escape.

"Yes, love, yes," he whispered against her lips, his warm breath fanning her increasing need for more.

His hand came to rest over her breast, creating in her the momentary belief that her breast had been formed for his hand to cup, imparting a wonderful sensation that melted her bones as heat melts candlewax.

But when he began pressing her gently back to lie on the blanket, a warning sprang into her mind, one of Cook's admonitions to Elsie that she had accidentally overheard.

" 'Tain't nothing wrong with a stolen kiss or two, mind ye. And a cuddle and feel won't harm ye. Just don't let him get ye down on yer back, or yer a goner."

Although Ashley wanted him to go on touching and kissing her, she did not wish to become "a goner." Whatever that might imply, she was certain it boded no good.

"No," she cried, pushing at him, trying to free herself.

For a moment or two she didn't think he meant to let her go, and her struggles grew more determined. When at last he released her, she was gasping for breath, her hair disheveled and her gown skewed up above her knees.

Embarrassed, humiliated, and angry, Ashley yanked at her gown, trying to set herself to rights. To her dismay, she heard the ominous sound of stitches ripping. Springing to her feet, she discovered the bodice had parted from the skirt almost a third of the way around the waist. She clutched at the gap and glared at Lord Damon.

"Look what you've done," she accused, finding herself addressing his back, because he had turned away and was brushing at his trews.

Swinging around, he examined her from toe to crown and smiled one-sidedly. "A sweet disorder in the dress," he murmured.

She frowned. "Do not attempt to smooth things over by quoting a poet."

He blinked. "I doubt Herrick would mind. I am sorry that *you* do, since the quote is most appropriate. However, I do apologize for the torn gown, though I regret nothing else."

Retaining enough wits to realize she was as put out at herself as she was annoyed with him, Ashley refrained from commenting on his words. Because the worry over how she could possibly explain the ripped waist to Mrs. Graham was foremost in her mind, she blurted, "I don't see how I shall be able to return home like this."

Pulling the white silk scarf from his neck, Lord Damon held it out to her. "Wrap this around you to hide the tear."

She took the scarf, and as she arranged it over the gap between bodice and skirt, thought that he did not understand how it would be even more difficult to try to explain away the scarf. Still, as a temporary measure, the scarf would hold up the skirt as well as conceal the condition of her gown from any who might observe her on the way home.

Ignoring her partly undone hair for the moment,

Ashley tried to decide how she was to put on her stockings in front of Lord Damon. Impossible!

She drew in her breath when he stepped close to her, reached up, and plucked several pins from her hair, completely loosening the already awry French twist. Curling auburn strands spilled over her shoulders. She backed away from him. "You had no right to do that," she said sharply.

"Ah, but I could not resist the chance to see your beautiful hair freed. Beauty is, after all, a woman's glory."

"As strength is a man's," she retorted tartly, relishing his quickly masked surprise that she had recognized the quote. Though she had not been taught the Greek language, Mrs. Mills had required her to read English translations.

"I shall not attempt to best you again," he said ruefully, as he began pulling on his boots.

She should never have been lured into accepting his company for one minute. If she had insisted he leave as soon as he appeared, he would not have kissed her and none of the rest would have occurred. How narrowly she had escaped being, like a strangled duck, a goner.

"To allow you the privacy you need," he said, stamping on the last boot, "I shall await you near the marsh."

Before she could protest that he need not wait for her anywhere because she did not wish his company, he left her. Grumbling, Ashley donned her stockings and slippers and tried to tame her unruly hair. Finally giving up, she tied on her bonnet, then folded the blanket and returned it to its cache, wondering if she would ever be able to return to her secret place, now forever imprinted with the memory of this time with Lord Damon.

The only article remaining was the hatbox containing the new straw bonnet brought by Lord Damon to replace the one she had lost in the river. She had not accepted it, but having been raised not to allow anything to go to waste, she could not bring herself to leave the box and hat behind.

If there had been another way to reach Mitred Bridge, she would have bypassed the marsh. Unfortunately, there was not, and Lord Damon joined her there.

"I have cogitated," he told her, "and have come up with the perfect solution."

"To what?" Her tone remained tart.

"To the torn gown. My horse is tethered near the bridge. We shall ride tandem to Lancaster Hall, where Aunt Tally's seamstress par excellence will solve your problem. I shall then commandeer the Hall's ancient conveyance and deliver you to your abode, providing the landau holds together for that long."

About to protest, Ashley paused. His plan would go a long way toward avoiding Mrs. Graham's scolding, for she would assume that Ashley had spent the morning with Lady Lancaster, not at all the same as being alone in her nephew's company.

"I fear my appearance will greatly shock your aunt," she protested.

"Aunt Tally enjoys rescuing strays. Your predicament will appeal to her sense of charity."

Although she did not appreciate being regarded

as a charitable cause, Ashley suppressed her indignation because she saw no other reasonable solution. When they came to where he had tethered his bay, he hung the hatbox from the saddle's gun sling and then lifted her onto the saddle, where she perched precariously, having chosen not to sit astride. He swung up, easing her half onto his lap, wrapping one arm around her waist. She could scarcely object, since she needed to be held securely on the horse.

The bay, whether because of the hatbox bouncing at his side or because he carried two instead of one, tended to be fractious, causing Ashley to cling to Lord Damon in a most unladylike fashion. Telling herself firmly it was preferable to risking a fall, she tried not to be aware of his warmth or his masculine scent, bemusing as both were.

Though it was some distance from Mitred Bridge, they seemed to reach Lancaster Hall in a trice—or so Ashley felt, being loath to have the journey end. Lord Damon was not only a phenomenon outside her experience and therefore to be relished, he was also the most fascinating man she had ever met. Never mind that he had behaved far too boldly—she should not have allowed him to.

They dismounted at the front of the house and a boy about Freddie's age but without the carrot-red hair came running from the stable to take the horse. Carrying the hatbox by its cord, Lord Damon ushered her into the Dower House, where she tried not to stare at the elegant surroundings.

"Where is my aunt, Langdon?" he asked the aged but still formidable butler who had opened the door.

"I believe Lady Lancaster is in the music room, sir."

Damon nodded and handed Langdon the hatbox.

As they followed the sound of a pianoforte to its source, Ashley caught glimpses of gold and white furniture in richly carpeted rooms, passing a tapestry depicting the Four Graces so exquisitely that she longed to stop and admire the work.

They entered the music room, also done in gold and white, just as the pianist, whom Ashley recognized as Lady Lancaster, was finishing a haunting Irish tune.

"Aunt Tally," Lord Damon said, advancing toward the piano with Ashley in his wake, "may I present Miss Ashley Douglas?"

Lady Lancaster rose. "My dear boy," she said, "there is no need to introduce Ashley. I have known her since she was a child." Turning to Ashley, she said, "How are you, my dear? I don't believe I have seen you since our village May Day festival, where, as I recall, you sang a lovely little Maying song about gathering rosebuds."

After murmuring a polite response, Ashley glanced at Lord Damon, hoping he would explain her presence here and saw that, for some reason, he looked confused and puzzled.

"Ashley has an excellent voice," Lady Lancaster went on to say. "Quite exceptional."

Lord Damon gazed from his aunt to Ashley and back at his aunt. "You know Miss Douglas?" he asked.

"Why should I not? Louth is a small village, and the shire itself is not populous. We are all acquainted with one another here."

"Did you not say 'since she was a child.'?" he persisted.

"Though I am not of the Methodist faith," Lady Lancaster told him, "I have always taken an interest in the welfare of the poor, benighted children in their orphanage. We all rejoiced when Ashley found a home with the Grahams. As my late husband often mentioned, Roland Graham is the salt of the earth."

"Did I hear the name Graham mentioned?" Liam Gounod's voice startled Ashley. She turned to see him standing in the doorway to the room. "The man who lost his boat?" He paused, then added, "I say, I've not interrupted a gathering, have I? Dreadfully sorry."

"Do come in, Liam," Lady Lancaster commanded. "I am not partial to people hovering in doorways."

"Sorry," Liam repeated, entering the room. His gaze fell on Ashley, and he smiled broadly. "The fair Miss Blayne," he exclaimed. "So Damon ran you to earth, did he? Delighted to see you again."

Lady Lancaster started to speak, paused, and frowned at Liam. "Miss Blayne?" she asked. "Are you addressing Miss Douglas?"

Liam blinked and shot a quick glance at Lord Damon. "Would swear she was Miss Alcida Blayne," he said. "The London songbird. Didn't recognize her at first myself, but Damon knew her cork out of the bottle."

Lady Lancaster turned her gaze on her nephew. "Since you introduced Ashley to me as Miss Douglas, I assume your mistake was put right by her."

Ashley shook her head in denial, an uncomfortable suspicion coiling within her. True, Lord Damon had called her Miss Douglas at the glen. But from what she had just heard, she concluded that at the secret pool, he had actually still believed her to be this London woman, as his remark about waltzing with her in London had indicated. No wonder he was stunned when his aunt revealed who she actually was.

What could possibly have been his reason for pretending to believe she was who she had claimed to be the previous day? Herself, in fact. The answer could only be to disarm her—or, actually, to disarm Alcida Blayne. But why? Recalling how she had permitted him to kiss her, Ashley flushed, doubly mortified to realize it had not been her at all; he had been kissing this Blayne woman. She wished she were anywhere else but here—anywhere except, perhaps, Humber's Harp.

" 'Tis obvious you are embarrassing Miss Douglas," Lady Lancaster scolded, advancing toward Ashley. "Come, child, we shall take our departure and leave these two gudgeons to suffer each other's company." Lady Lancaster grasped Ashley's arm and swept her from the room, up a curved staircase, and into a lavishly appointed bedchamber which did not appear to be in use. A white cat appeared out of nowhere, followed them into the room, and leaped onto the bed, curling itself into a ball.

Arranging herself comfortably in a wooden rocker whose seat was covered by a petit-point pillow, Lady Lancaster motioned to Ashley to be seated on a nearby green slipper chair. "Pray tell me, my dear," she said gently, "how this tangled coil came about."

Ashley did her best to be truthful without relating everything that had occurred. She could never, would never, admit to anyone how she had allowed Lord Damon to kiss her twice. "I have never heard of Miss Alcida Blayne," she finished, "so I cannot be certain she is a real person, though both Lord Damon and his friend behaved as though she were."

"I do not travel to London often enough to be aware of the latest singers or stage performers," Lady Lancaster said, "so I am unable to decide whether she exists or this flummery is merely a gammon on the part of my nephew and young Gounod. Let us put aside this Miss Blayne for a moment and tend to what I can set right." Reaching for a bellpull, she rang it.

"Polly," she said to the maid who appeared at the door, "please find a gown to fit Miss Douglas so she may change into it. My blue silk crape, perhaps, it has become a trifle snug of late."

When Polly hurried off to do her bidding, Lady Lancaster said, "Since my seamstress is not at the Hall today, I shall keep your gown until she arrives to mend it, then I shall arrange for the gown's return. I trust the blue crape will be a decent fit."

"You are most kind. I am very sorry to have arrived at the Hall looking like a tatterdemalion but Lord Damon insisted and he is somewhat difficult to deter."

Lady Lancaster smiled ruefully. "I fear he is a rapscallion. Bringing you here, however, was for the best. There is no need for Mrs. Graham to be distressed, as she certainly would have been had you arrived home with a strange gentleman's silk scarf about your waist and a torn gown underneath.

"I can easily believe your account of the events of

yesterday and this morning because I know my nephew. Whatever undergame he may be playing, he is not such a jingle-brained clodpole as to take advantage of a decent young girl on my very doorstep. But I suspect Mrs. Graham might misunderstand his motives—which I do admit appear rather murky."

"I cannot understand him at all," Ashley confessed.

"I do hope Mrs. Graham is not ailing," Lady Lancaster said. "I understand Mr. Mills has called twice at your home in the last two days."

Again today? Ashley thought in despair. No wonder I was allowed the day off. She wanted me gone from the house when he arrived with what could only be bad news as far as I was concerned.

Lady Lancaster leaned forward and touched her arm. "You appear distraught. Do let me know if Mrs. Graham is in need of my assistance. I should be only too glad to—"

"Mrs. Graham is fine, my lady," Ashley blurted. " 'Tis I who am not. His Grace is asking to have me live at Humber's Harp."

Lady Lancaster sat back in the rocker. "Good heavens, girl! Whatever for?"

"To teach Lady Clematis." She gazed unhappily at the older woman, who returned her look with concern.

"Oh, my dear, that will never do, a young girl like you. Surely Mr. Mills will say as much to the Grahams."

"I fear not." Ashley bit her lip. "I have refused too many offers, so 'tis time for me to earn my own way."

Lady Lancaster shook her head. "Not at Humber's

Harp. If I had a plumper pocket and did not already have a faithful companion in my cousin Harriet, I should take you on myself. I shall endeavor to think of another solution. Can you not find it in your heart to accept any of your suitors?"

"I wish I could, my lady." Ashley spoke plaintively.

"If Mr. Mills's advice is for you to become the girl's governess and the Grahams agree, you must try to delay your date of departure for as long as possible," Lady Lancaster said urgently. "In the meantime I shall do my best to find a more acceptable solution. No doubt Lady Clematis does need a governess, but perhaps someone older and more experienced . . ."

"Lord Damon was right about you," Ashley said. "You have a good heart."

Lady Lancaster shook her head. "Knowing him, I suspect his words were more on the order of telling you I have an unfortunate habit of collecting all kinds of strays and also of meddling. I try to do what good I can—often little enough. But one must keep trying to help—don't you agree?"

"I believe you have caught hold of a truth I had not given much thought to until the past few days."

"That is the way with most of us; we don't perceive such truths as lay before us until we ourselves land in predicaments we needs must be extricated from." Lady Lancaster sighed. After a moment she brightened. "I shall ask my nephew for advice in this matter. Here comes Polly with the gown now. She will help you change while I take Charles aside and confer with him."

Charles? Yes, Ashley recalled him introducing himself as Charles Jordon, Marquess of Damon. Freddie's advice to her to become Lord Damon's bit o' muslin echoed in her mind, making her wonder if that might not turn out to be milord's solution to her problem. If there *was* an Alcida Blayne in London, a songbird he was enamored of, and she resembled this woman, might he not be interested in Ashley Douglas for that reason? Interested enough in a look-alike to make her his fancy lady?

Ashley shook her head. She definitely did not wish to become any man's mistress!

She could see no easy way to deter her hostess from what she meant to do. In her way, the older woman was as stubborn as her nephew. But it was not beyond reason to believe that perhaps Charles Jordon, Marquess of Damon, was not at all the proper person for Lady Lancaster to consult about Ashley Douglas's immediate future.

Five

True to his word, once she was properly outfitted in a blue crape gown, Damon escorted Ashley home in his aunt's ancient landau. "I regret," he said formally, as he handed her into the creaking relic, "not to be able to offer you a decent hack. Unfortunately, my curricle is in London at the moment. We arrived in Mr. Gounod's, which at the moment has a sprung wheel under repair."

"Your aunt's carriage will suit nicely, Lord Damon." She did not so much as glance at him as she spoke. "Lady Lancaster has been most kind to me, and I am extremely grateful to her. I have no doubt that Mr. Graham will also be pleased to know that Mr. Gounod has recovered his boat and oars."

In other words, Damon thought, everyone is to be thanked except me. His one slim consolation was that his aunt had persuaded Ashley to accept the new straw bonnet as a partial apology for his shortcomings. Though Aunt Tally hadn't laid the whip on while Ashley was present, he knew he was in for a tongue lashing when he returned.

In the beginning, at least, he had done no worse than to make an honest mistake. He still had difficulty accepting that Ashley was not Alcida, for she bore a remarkable resemblance to the London singer. In retrospect, he realized Ashley's artless ways should have given him a clue, but then again, Alcida *was* an actress. All in all, though, it had been a harmless enough rig, as he was sure Liam would agree. Aunt Tally was a different kettle of fish.

"I *am* sorry," he said to Ashley. "I did not intend to embarrass you with my funning."

"I cannot think it well done of you," she said frostily.

No, he supposed she could not. "I don't believe we have set the neighborhood by the ear," he told her. "Rest assured your reputation will not be compromised, since I told Aunt Tally nothing more than that I had rescued a maiden in distress. No one will ever know about our time alone together in the glen."

She turned and glared at him. " 'Tis overmuch that *I* know."

Damn and blast, but she was a beauty. The silk gown his aunt had given her boasted a more fashionable neckline than her torn one, low enough to tantalize him with a view of the beginning swell of her breasts. Her flushed cheeks enhanced her delicate natural coloring as the blush had done at the pool, triggering his desire. Recalling how well she had fit into his arms fired an impulse to cup her face again and kiss her until she melted against him, as she had earlier today. Angry as she was, though, if he so much as touched her, the result was likely to be a resounding, well-deserved slap.

"You can be certain I shall do my utmost to forget I ever met you," she fumed.

He could not resist saying, "Ah, but will you be able to? For my part, I shall never forget being with you."

Her gloved hands fisted. "You are a scoundrel, sir!"

He smiled. "And you are well-nigh irresistible, my pretty Miss Douglas."

"I am not and never will be yours!"

If only she were not domiciled in his aunt's neighborhood, he might be tempted to take her words as a challenge. A dalliance with lovely Ashley would be the greatest of pleasures. But Aunt Tally would never countenance such a course, and so he could not, would not, even consider pursuing Ashley.

In which case, 'twould be wise to convince Liam to head back to London as soon as the wheel was repaired, thus placing himself beyond temptation. If he could not pick the unblemished country peach, in the city he could always reach for another, maybe not-quite-so-perfect one. Wasn't there a fair chance Alcida Blayne might be induced to share her charms with him?

"No, never," Ashley muttered, slanting him a dark glance.

Her words took him aback for a moment before he realized she could not possibly fathom his thoughts about Alcida and so must be referring to herself.

"Does that mean you will refuse me your first waltz?" he asked.

"I am as likely to waltz with you as I am to visit London."

Damon blinked at her tone, plaintive rather than

angry. "Surely, then, I have a chance," he said, "for everyone comes to London sooner or later."

She sighed. "I fear the only place I will be traveling to is—" She hesitated, then added, "much nearer home."

"I do not take your meaning."

"I should not have mentioned it. Pray, wipe my words from your mind."

In the glen, had she not spoken of being doomed? He started to ask her to explain, then shook his head, aware, after the way he had treated her, she was not likely to reveal anything to him. Young ladies of nineteen tended to dramatic outbursts. Quite possibly doomed meant no more than that she had been persuaded into becoming the bride of a man she disliked.

For some reason, the thought stuck in his craw. These rustic louts did not have the wits to appreciate her delicate beauty. Envisioning one of them pawing her made his gorge rise.

Caught up in his unpleasant imaginings, he was taken short when the landau slowed and stopped behind another rig in the drive of a two-story country cottage, roofed rather than thatched, obviously the home of a prosperous farmer. Flowering bushes and flowerbeds brightened the front of the dwelling.

"Mr. Mills is here." Ashley spoke in a hopeless tone, so softly he could barely hear her.

Mills? Who the devil—? Wait, wasn't Mills the local Methodist minister? Damon nodded to himself, the minister's presence confirming his idea that the Grahams must be strongly encouraging what they saw as an advantageous marriage for their foster daughter, a marriage she regarded as "doom."

"Don't go through with it, then," he said impulsively, laying his hand over hers. "Find a way out. You may have to search long and hard, but there always is another choice."

She stared at him, hope replacing the desolation in her eyes. "Do you really think so?"

He nodded, wishing he could offer her an acceptable alternative.

To his utmost surprise, she leaned to him and brushed her lips briefly over his in a butterfly kiss. "I forgive you for everything, Lord Damon," she murmured, as she pulled her hand from under his and prepared to leave. "You have inspired me and I shall find that choice."

Ephemeral as it was, Damon felt that kiss all the way back to Lancaster Hall.

Ashley entered by the front door, her thoughts so occupied with what Lord Damon had advised and her audacity in kissing him, that she started when Mrs. Graham materialized in the parlor door.

"There you are," Mrs. Graham said, then paused abruptly to look Ashley up and down, taking in the blue gown, the new bonnet, and the gloves Lady Lancaster had insisted on giving her. "Well," she said. "Well."

Ashley, feeling strangely lighthearted, almost repeated what Mr. Graham often said: *Well water's deep.* She caught back the words at the last minute, but offered no explanation for her change of attire.

"I do pray you have not disgraced us all," Mrs. Graham said, "but we shall discuss it later. I don't wish to keep Mr. Mills waiting. 'Tis unfortunate that Mr. Graham is not present but has gone downriver to retrieve his boat. However, it cannot be helped. You, at least, are here."

In the parlor, the minister reseated himself once Ashley and Mrs. Graham had sat down. He steepled his hands, cleared his throat, fixed his gaze on Ashley, and said, "As I have told Mrs. Graham, after conferring with His Grace's minister and discussing the matter with Mrs. Mills, as I do about the welfare of all our orphans, I have come to a decision. You are most fortunate, Ashley, to be offered the position of governess to Lady Clematis, and you must accept.

"I have been assured you will come to no harm at Humber's Harp. It appears that due to the shameless way his father flaunted his sins before his untimely death, gossip has tinged His Grace with an undeserved and false reputation. Since his wife passed away, he has become a rather solitary man, and people hereabouts have a regrettable tendency to equate solitude with dark deeds."

Ashley listened to every word the minister uttered and immediately discounted most of them. True, everyone agreed the old duke had been a four-bottle man, a fast and reckless driver and death on poachers. While no one accused the present duke of drinking to excess or endangering the neighborhood with his wild driving or putting the hapless poor to death over a rabbit they had ginned to feed hungry children, they attached darker sins to His Grace.

Remembering the rapacious gleam in his eyes

when he stared at her in the village, Ashley knew very well she would not be as safe at Humber's Harp as the minister would have her believe. Perhaps, after all, he did inherit what Ashley was not supposed to know about—the old earl's proclivity for bedding women.

She wondered uneasily what under heaven His Grace could have done to be accused of dark deeds. Putting that unsettling question aside for the moment, she carefully selected an answer for Mr. Mills, one that would allow her to delay her departure.

"I realize I should be grateful to be offered a chance such as this," she told him. "However, I do need some time to get ready." Turning to Mrs. Graham, she said, "I think you will agree that my wardrobe is hardly suitable for Humber's Harp."

Mrs. Graham blinked, then nodded. " 'Tis true what Ashley says," she told Mr. Mills. "We must have some gowns run up for her."

The minister offered a wintery smile. "I am pleased you have come to your senses, Ashley. Mrs. Mills thought you would. 'A dreamer,' she said, 'and at the same time able to see what must be done.' Dreams are all very well, but they do not make the world go round."

I have his approval, so I shall strike while the iron is hot, Ashley decided. Surely he must relent and reveal what he has held back for all these years.

"Will you not tell me now what I have asked you so many times?" she begged. "I know you and Mrs. Mills chose my last name, but did you also choose my first name?"

Mr. Mills cleared his throat. "We do not wish to

advance false hopes for our orphaned children," he said, as he had so many other times. "Still—" He paused and fixed his gaze on the window while Ashley held her breath.

"Since you have proved you are a young lady who understands what must be done for her own good," he said finally, "I see no harm in telling you what little I know. You came to us when you were three, and very ill, I might add. Indeed, despite our prayers, we despaired of your recovery. When it became clear you would live, Mrs. Mills told me she believed you must be a special kind of person, which is why you received from her a more than adequate education. Her scheme was to prepare you for what she thought would be a unique role in life."

Ashley could hardly believe her ears. A special person? No one had ever said those words to her.

"As you can see, your education will be of considerable use in teaching Lady Clematis," he continued.

"Yes, I understand. I have always been grateful to Mrs. Mills for the interest she took in me. And," she added hastily, "to you as well."

He nodded in acknowledgment. "As for your name, 'Ashley' was engraved inside a small heart-shaped locket made of gold, attached to a gold chain around your neck. We could not be certain whether or not Ashley was a family name, so we decided to use it as your given name. We planned to return the locket and chain to you when you married. As it is, we shall present you with them before you leave for Humber's Harp."

"A gold locket?" she managed to say, her mind in a whirl. No one had ever mentioned she had arrived at the orphanage with anything but the clothes she had on.

"Exactly. Gold. Which is why we waited until you were of an age to understand that the locket is a valuable keepsake to be guarded rather than worn."

A keepsake from someone who cared enough about her to place a gold locket around her neck. Her mother? Ashley blinked back tears. I shall cherish my name as much as the locket, she told herself, for now I know my name truly belongs to me.

The seamstress Mrs. Graham patronized, Mrs. Teasdale, the Mrs. a courtesy title because of her advanced age, arrived two days later. As Ashley endured the seemingly endless measurings and fittings, she observed the seamstress with particular, if covert, interest. Thin to the point of being gaunt, Mrs. Teasdale, actually a Miss because she was a spinster, appeared to be withering a little more every year, like an apple left on the tree over many winters.

Shall I be like her one day? Ashley asked herself. I am already nineteen and have not yet met a man I wish to marry.

As if in contradiction, the memory of Lord Damon's kisses and caresses floated into her mind, sending a delicious frisson tingling through her. She sighed, aware of the futility of dreaming of him. He had left for London the day after their secret meeting in the glen. Quite probably they would never meet again.

"I shall be finished in a trice," Mrs. Teasdale said, mistaking her sigh for one of weariness.

"There is no need to hurry," Ashley assured her. Indeed, the longer the seamstress took to make the three gowns, the longer Ashley could delay leaving for Humber's Harp.

"By all accounts, His Grace is an impatient man, not one to be kept waiting," Mrs. Teasdale said.

Ashley fingered the dove gray cotton material being fitted to her. "Perhaps. But I can hardly assume my position with a deficient wardrobe."

"With these three and the gowns you already have, you total six, which should be sufficient to keep you for some time. I pray you will not send for me after you take up residence at Humber's Harp, for I have no wish to set foot in that dark hall."

Ashley raised her chin. "The Reverend Mr. Mills assures me I shall be in no danger there."

Mrs. Teasdale stopped what she was doing and, narrowing her faded blue eyes, looked directly at Ashley. "Do you know why the name of Roxton Hall was changed?"

"Was it not always Humber's Harp?"

"Indeed, 'twas not." Mrs. Teasdale glanced around, then eased down onto a tapestry stool. "John Humber was the first Duke of Roxton, way back around the time of the troubles. He favored Charles I, and like his king, was beheaded for his loyalty. Those who know say that before he died, this first duke bargained with the devil and received a golden harp to seal the pact."

Ashley stared at her wide-eyed. "What was the pact?"

"Why, that he should not die."

"Did you not say he was beheaded?"

The seamstress nodded. "In the courtyard, for all to see. Yet to this day John Humber, First Duke of Roxton, walks at night in his manor house and plays the devil's music on that golden harp."

"A ghost?" Despite herself, Ashley's voice quivered. Was she destined to contend with a ghost as well as Thomas Farrington, the Eighth Duke of Roxton?

"Some say a ghost, some believe he is John Humber in the flesh." The seamstress rose and resumed her work. "I could not, in good faith, watch you go there without warning you."

Aware Mrs. Teasdale meant well, Ashley murmured her thanks while fervently wishing she had never heard the grisly tale.

"About the blue silk crape," the seamstress said. "Mrs. Graham wishes me to sew a lace insert into the neckline of the bodice. A shame, since 'tis the most fashionable gown you own. Would you prefer to have me make a fichu instead?"

Aware her three new gowns were to have high necklines by Mrs. Graham's decree, Ashley nodded. A fichu could be removed if she cared to do so. Although where she was going, she might well never want to.

Five days later, the gowns were finished. Mrs. Teasdale departed with a speaking look directed at Ashley as she said her farewells, a reminder of what lay ahead. Refusing to dwell on revenants playing ghostly music, Ashley, wearing the mended green gown Lady Lancaster had sent back, fled the house. She had delayed as long as she could—where was she to find this alternate choice Lord Damon had dangled before her?

If he had offered to take her to London and set her up as his bit o' muslin, would she have agreed? Pondering this question, Ashley wandered down the lane toward the village, so intent on whether or not she would have chosen to become his fancy lady that she only belatedly became aware that her thumbs were pricking. A change? No longer certain a change was necessarily for the better, she slowed her steps and stopped. What now?

The trill of a meadowlark caught her ear and she turned toward the field. Was the bird a sign? Searching for the lark, she was not aware of Freddie hurrying toward her until he spoke.

"Miss Ashley!" he cried. "I got something for ye."

"What is it?"

" 'Tis a note." He waved a folded piece of paper at her.

From Lord Damon! was her first excited thought, as she reached for the paper.

As she unfolded it, Freddie rattled on. "Was in Louth, I was, took the gray mare to Luddy the smith. Waiting for 'er to be shoed, I was, 'n' the Inn 'ostler come in, Sandy by name. Got a message for ye to give Miss Douglas, 'e says. So I run to find ye."

Having read what was on the paper, Ashley looked at Freddie in puzzlement, wondering if the note could possibly be from Lord Damon. "This says I should come to the Harp and Whistle as soon as I can, 'tis a matter of life and death. There is no signature. How can I tell who wrote it?"

And did she dare go to the Inn if, by chance, Lord

Damon was the writer? If she did, her reputation would be ruined beyond all recall.

"What if a man wrote the note?" she added.

Freddie shook his head. "Sandy says 'twas a lady staying at the Inn. Dressed all in black, 'e told me, with a black veil so ain't nobody seen 'er face. Got a cough, she 'as, 'n' 'e thinks maybe she ain't long for this world."

"Who can she be?" Ashley asked, completely at a loss.

Freddie shook his head. "Ye coming? I got to go back 'n' get the mare.

"Of course I'm coming! I cannot ignore such a heartfelt plea."

She was glad of Freddie's presence when she entered the Harp and Whistle. As a rule, ladies did not go into inns unaccompanied by a man and, stableboy or not, Freddie *was* a male.

"Please tell me where I can find the lady who is staying here," she asked the proprietor.

"Dressed all in black, she is," the irrepressible Freddie put in.

Directed to the room at the top of the stairs, Ashley climbed with Freddie trailing behind her. She stopped at the door, raised her hand to tap on the wood, then held. If this was the predicted change, what was she letting herself in for?

"Ain't ye gonna knock?" Freddie asked. " 'Ere, I'll do it for ye." He banged on the door with his fist.

For long moments there was no response. Freddie was preparing to knock again when they heard the bolt being drawn. The door opened to reveal a veiled woman, her head and face completely covered.

"Thank God!" she exclaimed, reaching for Ashley. "It really *is* you."

Before Ashley could move or speak, the woman collapsed against her. With Freddie's help, Ashley managed to half-carry, half-drag the lady in black inside the room and lift her onto the bed. As she did so, the veil twisted to one side, revealing the woman's face and a strand of auburn hair.

"Rats and mice!" Freddie cried, staring from the unconscious woman to Ashley and back. "If she ain't the spitting image of ye."

Six

Though Ashley's mind roiled with questions—who was this mysterious lady in black, and what was she doing at the Harp and Whistle?—she set her curiosity aside while she tended to the obviously ill woman. Carefully, so as not to hurt her, Ashley slipped off the woman's veil and head covering, reasoning that the veil might hamper her breathing. Curly auburn tresses spilled onto the pillow and the woman's eyelids fluttered.

"Want me to go for the doctor?" Freddie asked.

The woman's green eyes opened. "No doctor," she whispered. Gazing up at Ashley, she smiled weakly and raised her hand. "I cannot believe you are real."

Ashley took hold of the offered hand, finding it feverishly hot. She started to ask the woman's name, but before the words left her mouth, she realized she knew. "Alcida," she said. "You are Alcida Blayne, you are a real live person, after all."

"I am amazed that you know. At the moment, I scarce feel alive, and only the Alcida is real. I will show you." She pulled her hand away to fumble with a chain around her neck, sliding around a locket that had slipped to the back, a gold, heart-shaped locket.

Ashley held her breath as the woman opened it.

Leaning forward she read what was inscribed inside. "Alcida," she murmured. There was no doubt in her mind the locket Mr. Mills had said was hers would be identical except for the name inside.

Alcida tried to sit up and failed, flopping back down onto the pillows while Ashley gazed worriedly at her, alarmed at her weakness.

"Be ye twins?" Freddie asked.

Alcida nodded. Even that slight effort appearing to tire her, for she closed her eyes.

Of course they were twins, Ashley told herself. "No wonder Lord Damon was confused," she blurted, before she could stop herself.

Alcida spoke without opening her eyes. "Of course, that is how you knew my name—he mistook you for me. And that is why I came here. The *on-dit* in London has you pushing him into the river. I came to Louth because of that story, hoping against hope to find you at last. I have searched so long." She beat a weak fist against the mattress. "If only I had not acquired this miserable fever."

"You are far too ill to remain at the Harp and Whistle," Ashley said.

"Gonna bring 'er home to Master 'n' Missus?" Freddie asked.

About to tell him yes, Ashley paused, a sinking feeling inside her as she remembered she was due to leave for Humber's Harp in the morning. She doubted that Mrs. Graham would permit another delay to allow her to nurse her twin back to health. That meant, at best, Alcida would be left behind for Mrs. Graham to take care of. How could she gain a twin sister only to leave her?

My twin. She savored the words. She had a sister, an identical sister; Alcida was her true family. Somehow, she must find a way to take care of her.

"I fear Mrs. Graham will not be pleased," Ashley said unhappily.

"If I was ye," Freddie said, "afore ye make plans, me, I'd ask Lady Lancaster what to do. She 'elps everybody."

Ashley stared at him. "Lady Lancaster? I could not."

"Seems like ye ain't got much choice, seeing as 'ow ye'll be in devil's clutches come morning."

Alcida's eyes flew open. "The devil? Who is going to the devil?"

"Miss Ashley," Freddie volunteered.

Ashley put Humber's Harp from her mind and tried to think what to do. Could she ask the Millses to help? Recalling that Mrs. Mills had been far from well lately with her heart problem, she shook her head. It would not be fair. Yet she was determined not to allow Alcida to stay one more minute longer at the inn. Reluctantly, she decided Freddie was right about her choices. There was only one. Much as she hated to, she would have to throw herself upon Lady Lancaster's mercy again.

Once she had made the decision, she marshalled her forces. "Freddie, you collect the gray mare from the smith and tell him Miss Ashley needs to borrow a rig. Bring mare and rig here and we will carry Miss Alcida down to it and travel to Lancaster Hall. Do not tell a soul who she is, do you hear?"

"Cross me 'eart, I ain't gonna breathe a word," Freddie told her solemnly, his forefinger making an

X across his chest. He took one last wondering look at Alcida before hurrying off.

Turning to her twin sister, she sat on the edge of the bed and took Alcida's hot, dry hand in hers. "We are going to Lancaster Hall," she said.

"Lancaster Hall," Alcida murmured. "Lord Damon visits there, but he is in London."

" 'Tis his aunt, Lady Lancaster, we wish to see. She will find a way to help you get well."

"If you say so. I realize I cannot remain at this inn. No need to deal with the innkeeper; the room has been paid for. Put my veil back on before we leave, 'twill avoid gossip. No one here has seen what I look like except you and the boy, and I see nothing to be gained by revealing my identity to all and sundry." Alcida closed her eyes again, spent merely from talking.

Understanding how village gossip would run rampant because she had come to the Harp and Whistle and took the mysterious woman in black to Lancaster Hall, Ashley agreed silently with Alcida's wish to remain veiled. How much more the villagers would have on their plates if they also discovered she and Alcida were twins.

While Alcida fell into a feverish doze, Ashley packed her twin's belongings into the bag Alcida had brought with her from London. When Freddie raced up the stairs to announce the horse and rig awaited, Ashley had him take the bag down first. Rousing Alcida, she managed to get the veil and head covering into place before he returned.

When it became obvious that Alcida was too weak to walk, even with help, Ashley and Freddie fashioned a seat for her with their crossed hands and carried her down, lifting her into the rig with some difficulty. Alcida slumped against the seat, propped up by Ashley, sitting next to her.

"Drive," Ashley ordered, and Freddie clucked to the gray mare until she ambled away, leaving behind a number of gawking spectators.

When they finally arrived at Lancaster Hall, Ashley took a moment to summon up her nerve before alighting from the rig. I am doing this for my sister, she told herself firmly, as she hurried to the front door.

When Langdon opened it, she took a deep breath and said, "I must see Lady Lancaster."

"I shall inquire, Miss Douglas," he informed her, allowing her to enter and indicating a tiny room off the entry.

Ashley, far too agitated even to enter the room, much less be aware of her surroundings, paced up and down in the entry until Langdon returned with Lady Lancaster trotting at his heels.

"Do come in, child," she said. "Langdon told me that you appeared overwrought, and I see he was correct. Whatever is the trouble?"

"My twin sister is outside in a rig," Ashley cried, "and she is terribly ill with a fever. I must go to Humber's Harp in the morning to begin my governess duties there. How can I help her? I don't know what to do." To her distress, her voice broke on the last few words. She made a desperate attempt to blink back the threatening tears.

"Langdon will see that she is taken care of for the moment," Lady Lancaster said soothingly, putting an arm around Ashley. "While he is doing so, you will come into the morning room with me and explain everything, beginning with this twin sister. I was not aware you had one."

In the morning room, Ashley poured out her story, mixing in her fear of Humber's Harp along with how Alcida had sent her a note from the Harp and Whistle. "She heard London gossip about the mistake your nephew made, thinking I was Alcida Blayne," she finished, "and that is why she came to Louth, hoping to find me."

A tap on the door made her pause. Langdon entered and said, "The young lady is quite ill, Milady. I believe you would wish her to be under a doctor's care, so I have taken the liberty of sending for him."

"Excellent," Lady Lancaster told him. "I can always count on you."

Langdon shifted his attention to Ashley. "Miss Douglas, your young stable lad seems most anxious about returning the mare to his employers and the rig to the village."

"Oh, dear," Ashley said, "I don't know what to tell Freddie to do."

Lady Lancaster began issuing orders. "See to it that the horse and rig are returned, Langdon. Perhaps it would be well to keep the boy—Freddie, is it?—here at the Hall until I decide what I intend to do about this coil. I shall compose a note to the Grahams that can be delivered when the mare is brought to them."

"Very good, Milady."

"Please tell Freddie I shall talk to him shortly," Ashley put in.

Langdon nodded and exited.

After asking a few questions, Lady Lancaster said, "I believe I have it sorted out. You say no one except you and Freddie have seen your sister's face?"

"That is correct, my lady. She wore a dark veil at all times at the Inn, and she was wearing the veil when we arrived here."

Lady Lancaster nodded. "I shall inform the doctor, when he arrives, that Miss Ashley Douglas has suddenly come down with a fever. He will then believe he is treating you. I shall write a note in the same vein to the Grahams and to the duke. Obviously, you cannot go to Humber's Harp while you lie ill in bed. You will don the black gown and veil your sister wore and become my mysterious London visitor. How bright is this stable lad?"

Ashley, still reeling from Lady Lancaster's announcement of the switch in identities, made an effort to pull herself together so she could answer. "Freddie? He is an orphan, as I am. He did not come from the Millses, so he is unschooled, but he is usually one step ahead of everyone else. He is—" Ashley hesitated for a moment, wondering if she dared reveal the truth. Finally deciding to, no matter what Lady Lancaster might think, she added, "Freddie and I are friends."

"Good. If he is intelligent, he should have no difficulty comprehending our plan and he will want to keep the secret to protect you, his friend."

"The plan," Ashley said, trying to be certain she understood it herself. "I wish we did not have to deceive the Grahams—they will worry about me being ill."

"No doubt." Lady Lancaster did not sound sorry

or apologetic. "On the other hand, they were apparently quite ready to send an innocent off to Humber's Harp, of all places, without a qualm. Since you have brought up the Grahams, however, I am reminded that we shall have to avoid them arriving on my doorstep." She thought for a moment or two, then asked, "Have you ever had the measles?"

Mystified, Ashley shook her head.

"Then the measles it is," Lady Lancaster said. "I would think the Grahams would be somewhat reassured by that diagnosis, since most recover from the disease. We will insist no one can enter the room lest they contract the measles. So—no visitors. Except for the doctor for you, as the mysterious lady in black, and for me.

"But will not the doctor—?"

Lady Lancaster cut her off with a raised hand. "I shall speak to Dr. Higgins. There will be no problem." She reached for the bell cord and rang.

When Langdon appeared, she briefly outlined the plan, swearing him to secrecy. "Do bring Freddie here," she told him, when she had finished. "We can afford no leaky spouts if we are to succeed."

Freddie, perched uneasily on the edge of a straight-backed chair because Lady Lancaster had ordered him to sit, listened wide-eyed to her explanation of what was to be done and to her admonitions of secrecy.

"Won't say a word, ma'am," he promised, in the most subdued tone Ashley had ever heard him use. "Wouldn't do nothing to 'urt Miss Ashley, I wouldn't. Me mummer's dubbed for good 'n' all."

"He means his mouth is closed," Ashley put in hastily.

Lady Lancaster smiled. "How would you like to go to London, Freddie?" she asked.

"Rats and mice!" he cried. "London? Give me right arm, I would, ma'am."

Ashley stared from him to Lady Lancaster, wondering what new scheme had entered the older woman's head.

"If events unfold as I hope, you shall do just that," Lady Lancaster told him. "And you shan't have to sacrifice an arm. For now, though, we must arrange for Miss Douglas to masquerade as her sister. Do you think you could nip up the back stairs? Langdon will be waiting in the upstairs hall outside a door. Bring whatever he hands you to this room."

As Freddie shot through the door, Lady Lancaster said, "He is an appealing lad and will make a passable footman for you."

Freddie, a footman? For her? "I don't believe I understand," she said.

Lady Lancaster leaned over and patted her hand. "You will, my dear, once your sister is quite recovered, as I am sure she will be soon. I have heard identical twins tend to mimic each other in every way. Since you have enjoyed good health all your life, I would hazard she has as well. Which means she should throw off her fever and be back on her feet in no time. I quite look forward to meeting my nephew's London songbird."

Lord Damon's songbird? What with the shock of meeting a twin sister she did not know existed and finding that sister feverishly ill, Ashley had completely forgotten what he and Liam Gounod had said about Alcida. A singer on the London stage.

But not *his,* Ashley told herself, not Lord Damon's. When he had believed her to be Alcida, he had not behaved as though Alcida was his fancy lady. Indeed, he had seemed to be courting her, if courting was the proper word for his most improper behavior.

Freddie returned with Alcida's bag and was sent off to guard the ill woman's door. "Quite natural, since you are her devoted servant," Lady Lancaster told him, before he went out. "It shall be your duty for as long as she is ill to see that no one enters the room except for the doctor, Langdon, or us."

"You shall take your meals with me," Lady Lancaster told Ashley as she helped her, in lieu of a maid, into one of Alcida's several identical black gowns. "I fear you will have to practice eating with the veil in place, since you will not be able to remove it. Your presence at the table will certainly titillate all the servants. I shall have to come up with a logical reason for the veil's constant presence."

Still dazed by Lady Lancaster's adept maneuvering of those around her, Ashley had no doubt the older woman would find a reason, logical or not, to end all reasons.

When she was properly gowned and veiled, Lady Lancaster, carrying Ashley's green gown in a bundle, led the way up to the bedchamber Alcida had been taken to. Alcida, her eyes closed, lay in a white and gold four-poster bed draped with white netting.

"I detest mosquitos," Lady Lancaster said, referring to the netting. "Unfortunately, Lincolnshire marshes do breed them." she lifted a folded garment from the basin stand. "You might wish to help your sister into the nightgown Langdon has laid out for her."

Lady Lancaster stood back while Ashley did just that. Alcida had made a weak effort to help and it had obviously exhausted her, for she once again lay with her eyes closed.

Lady Lancaster moved to the bedside, leaned over, peered intently into Alcida's face, straightened and looked at Ashley. "I assume her eyes are as green as yours?"

Ashley nodded.

Giving a satisfied nod, Lady Lancaster said, "Then once she recovers, if she agrees to cooperate, my plan should prove to be an unqualified success."

Ashley, intent on how her sister was faring, scarce heard her. Noting a basin of water on the stand, she dipped the accompanying cloth into the water, wrung it out, and placed the cool, damp cloth on Alcida's forehead. Her sister opened her eyes.

"Yes," Lady Lancaster said, "the exact same shade of green. A remarkable resemblance." She reached for Alcida's hand and took it in both of hers. "Do not feel you must speak," she said. "I am Lady Lancaster, and you, as Ashley's sister, are welcome in my house. I realize you are feverish, but do you think your head is clear enough for you to hear me out?"

Alcida's "Yes, my lady" was a mere whisper.

"The reason she is dressed in black, as you were, is because she is Alcida for the time the two of you remain in my house. She is Alcida and you are Ashley. Try to remember—*you are Ashley*. We needs must create this masquerade to save your sister, a true innocent, from a dreadful fate, which I will explain when you are feeling better. To keep visitors away, we are saying your illness is the measles. I realize this is not the case and so will Dr. Higgins, who will be along shortly to treat you, believing you are Ashley Douglas. The doctor is an old friend who will not quibble about what I choose to call your fever. Do you understand?"

"I am Ashley," Alcida murmured. "Ashley is Alcida."

"Very good. I shall leave you with your sister, who will be taking care of you." She released Alcida's hand, laid it back on the coverlet, and patted it, saying, "Rest and get well quickly."

After Lady Lancaster left, Alcida asked, "What is she up to?"

Ashley shook her head. "Pray, don't worry about it now. However odd her plan may sound, she is trying to help us both."

When the doctor arrived, he diagnosed the illness as marsh fever, common in Lincolnshire. "Miss Ashley," he told the woman in the bed, after removing a bottle of red liquid from his bag, "take a dram of this three times a day and I predict you will be as right as rain in less than a fortnight."

Lady Lancaster and the doctor proved to be correct in their prediction of a speedy recovery. Two days later, the sick woman insisted on getting out of bed and, well-wrapped against a chill, was allowed to sit in a chair by the window of the bedchamber.

"Do pull up a chair and sit next to me," Alcida begged. "And do take off that hideous veil for a few moments. I am weary of looking at it instead of your face. Freddie is such a good watchdog that no one will enter who is not already in on the masquerade."

Ashley did as she asked, sitting opposite her at the window, out of sight of anyone who might look up. She was becoming accustomed to the reality of having a twin sister and was thrilled that she and Alcida were growing closer each day. How wonderful to see her sister regaining her health.

"Up until this moment, you have declared me too ill to speak of our mutual past," Alcida said, "but you cannot deny I am all but recovered."

Nodding, Ashley said, "I admit to the most intense curiosity. You knew I existed while I had no clue about you. Have you been with our mother?"

"No longer than you were—that is, until we were three years of age and she met Count Roulais. Mother, an exceptionally beautiful widow, had resisted all offers, but by then was on her uppers and desperate. She could see no way to support us and herself other than agreeing to the count's proposal because she was too much of a lady to consider becoming any man's mistress' and he was the first man who had agreed to marry her. She did not like the two conditions he set up, one being that they would live in France, the other that though he would provide well for us, she could not take us with her when they left England because he found children a nuisance."

"How do you know all this?" Ashley asked wonderingly.

"Count Roulais told me himself, after Mother died when we were twelve. He made a special trip to England to find us, not certain he could because he knew the arrangements made for us when they married and left the country went awry almost before they crossed the Channel.

"For some never determined reason, we did not go to live in Kent with Mother's nanny. Perhaps she died; the count did not know. Instead, we were separated. A music hall actress took me in, so I remained in London where the count eventually found me, after spotting me on the stage with my foster mother, whose last name was Blayne. He searched for you, but there was no clue to your whereabouts."

"Someone unknown placed me in a Lincolnshire Methodist orphanage," Ashley said. "The Grahams took me in when I was twelve."

"The year Mother died." Alcida reached for Ashley's hand and squeezed it. "I wish I could remember her, but I cannot."

"Nor can I. I always hoped to find my family, but I did not even know I had a locket like yours until the Methodist minister told me about it a few days ago. He was waiting until I married to give the locket to me, as he considered it too valuable to be in a child's possession."

Alcida frowned. "Did you not mention to me that you had turned down marriage offers?"

Ashley made a face. "Every one. In lieu of marriage, I am to become a governess. In fact, had you not arrived and sent me that note, I would be at Humber's Harp this very moment."

"Why do I associate that name with the devil? Perhaps from some feverish dream?"

Ashley hesitated, then, deciding not to keep anything from her twin, said, "I am to teach Lady Clema-

is, the daughter of Thomas Farrington, the Eighth Duke of Roxton. He is not well thought of in these parts. They suspect him of dealing with the devil, as his ancestor, the first duke, is supposed to have done."

"How interesting. Does he?"

Alcida's words took Ashley aback, since she did not consider trafficking with the devil at all interesting. Quite the opposite. "I don't know whether he does or not," she said, "though I think it rather unlikely. What fills me with apprehension is the way he looked at me when he saw me in the village."

Her sister smiled wryly. "One of *those* gentlemen. I have discouraged more of them than I care to count in London. Despite my profession, which needs must encourage flirting with the gentlemen, I fear I am like our mother. 'Tis marriage or nothing for me."

She eyed Ashley levelly. "Lady Lancaster called you an innocent, did she not? Now that I am coming to know you, I am sure she is quite correct. That being so, I believe I am beginning to catch a glimmer of her ingenious, completely devious hum. What a clever lady."

Seven

Once Alcida was on her feet, she quickly regained her strength, refusing to be confined to the bedchamber. She and Ashley, who was still veiled and garbed in black, took a walk each day in the gardens, while they exchanged life stories.

"I don't think I told you that Count Roulais passed away last year," Alcida said, as they strolled among the roses.

Ashley absently snipped off a withered red rose with her thumb and forefinger, discarding the disintegrating petals on the gardener's compost heap. "You did not mention that fact," she said.

"So you do not yet know that in the end, he must have sincerely regretted what he had done to us. I do believe his guilt over refusing to allow us to live with him and Mother caused him to try to make up for whatever hardships we may have suffered. Otherwise, why would he, in his will, leave us each a generous dowry? Not only that, he also settled on us, for when we shall turn twenty-one, a decent enough yearly sum to be kept in each of our names even after we marry."

"*If* we marry," Ashley corrected. She sighed. "I realize it was thoughtful of the count, and I am grateful to know my future is assured. Still, I cannot think kindly of him."

" 'Tis difficult, I agree, for he cost us our mother. As for marriage, I am none too certain about it myself. And our assured future, alas, is two years away, so we must earn our way in the world until then. Because I refuse to become a gentleman's plaything, I am far from plump in the pocket. I was left my foster mother's small house, purchased for her by one of her admirers, as such gentlemen are called. If not for that, I should have great difficulty in finding the money to pay rent. Nor can I afford a maid, although I am fortunate enough to have acquired a companion who insists on acting as my housekeeper.

"Ursula was a dresser at the theaters, a friend of my foster mother's. When Mrs. Blayne died, Ursula arrived on my doorstep and never left, despite the fact I cannot pay her. What I would have done without her I do not know. I should like above all to have you come to live with me, but I fear you would have to find employment, too, for us to be able to scrape along. We shall hear Lady Lancaster out before we make any decisions."

"Hear her out?"

"Are you not aware she has something up her sleeve that concerns our welfare?"

Considering the matter, Ashley recalled various remarks of Lady Lancaster's that had made little sense to her. "You may be right but she has confessed to me that she is far from wealthy herself. What can she do?"

"Even on this short an acquaintance with her," Alcida said, "I have come to the conclusion that the lady is seldom at a loss. We shall wait and see."

Seated in morning room on the tenth day after her arrival at Lancaster Hall, Alcida declared to Lady Lancaster and Ashley that she felt as fit as a fencer. Glancing at the older woman, she added, "I use the term deliberately, my lady, because I sense that you may soon expect me to perform as agilely as an experienced fencer."

Lady Lancaster nodded. "I pass no judgment, my dear, but I cannot help but believe your London stage experience must have forced you to become extremely capable in dealing with the male of the species. Whereas Ashley—" She broke off and sighed.

Ashley stared from one to the other, understanding they were referring to Lady Lancaster's still unannounced scheme. Alcida had hinted she might know what it was but she had steadfastly refused to reveal what she suspected to Ashley, saying, " 'Tis her plan, not mine. She will tell us in her own time what she has in store for us."

"Ashley sings very well, does she not?" Lady Lancaster asked Alcida. "I have heard you in duet and find my ear cannot separate your voices."

"Her voice is not the problem," Alcida replied.

"I understand. Still, I gather she whistled my nephew down the wind, a not inconsiderable feat for a country miss."

"So Mr. Gounod has been telling all who will listen."

Exasperated by them speaking of her as though

she were not present, Ashley said tartly, "Am I to be a part of this or not?"

Both turned to her. Lady Lancaster spoke first. "Would you not like to visit London, my dear?"

"My lady, that is the same question you posed to Freddie not long past," Ashley said. "My answer would be as enthusiastic as his. But I know 'tis not possible because I must soon take up my duties as—"

"Dear sister," Alcida interrupted, "have you not yet guessed the truth? You are not going to Humber's Harp to be gobbled up by His Grace." She stood, threw out her arms to strike a pose, and exclaimed, "You are gazing at Lady Clematis's new governess."

Ashley gaped at her. "You? How can that be possible?"

Alcida raised her eyebrows. "Because, as you must know, I am Miss Ashley Douglas, in person, cured in record time of the measles by Dr. Higgins's foul-tasting concoction. You, there behind that somber veil, are Miss Alcida Blayne, the London songbird."

"Such is the essence of my plan," Lady Lancaster admitted modestly.

Everything fell into place for Ashley and she bemoaned her lack of wit in not fathoming earlier what was in the wind. She was not usually such a goose. "I cannot allow you to place yourself in danger," she told Alcida firmly.

Alcida tossed her head, her auburn curls dancing. "Pish, tosh, and piffle. I shall not be in the slightest peril. I intend to teach His devilish Grace a well-deserved, long-overdue lesson. You are the one who will have to watch your step in London. Fortunately, Ursula is a dragon when it comes to protecting the innocent."

"Freddie will also be at your side," Lady Lancaster put in, "as your devoted young footman. As you pointed out to me, the lad misses very little. Langdon believes Freddie will go far, and he is never wrong."

"But I—"

Lady Lancaster held up her hand. "No protests. 'Tis settled. That being so, you two must be off to the secret pool in the glen where you, Alcida, will help Ashley practice your London routines without anyone around to hear."

"Secret pool?" Alcida echoed.

To her dismay, a vision of wading in the pool with Lord Damon flashed into Ashley's head and her face grew so hot she feared she had turned as red as a sailor's delight sunset.

Eyeing her, Alcida commented, "Perhaps not so far down the wind as you believe, my lady."

"At the time, my nephew thought she was you, even though he pretended to believe her claim that she was Ashley Douglas. 'Twas quite a twisted coil."

"True." Ashley's agreement was heartfelt.

Alcida smiled at her, prompting Lady Lancaster to gasp. "Oh, dear, I have just observed one difference in the two of you. As I recall, Ashley's dimple is in her left cheek, while yours, Alcida, is in your right."

"Lift up your veil and smile," Alcida ordered.

Ashley obeyed.

"A perfect mirror image," Lady Lancaster said. "His Grace will be none the wiser, but how about the many people who have watched the London songbird perform?"

"I do color my cheeks and sometimes affect a beauty spot," Alcida said. "Because of that, I cannot believe the misplaced dimple will prove to be a problem for Ashley."

"We shall not fret over it," Lady Lancaster declared. "You are so alike otherwise that anyone who might notice will be convinced he or she was mistaken as to the dimple's exact location."

"I still am not convinced this switch in identities should be done," Ashley protested.

"Of course it should," Alcida told her. "And will. You will be far safer in London with Ursula, the Dragon Lady and Freddie looking out for you than alone in Humber's Harp, with a man reputed to be the devil's own and quite probably lecherous as well. You would be terrified of him, a quivering victim, while I shall enjoy the challenge of outwitting Thomas Farrington, Eighth Duke of Roxton."

"Would it not be wiser for me to return to London with you and seek employment as a governess there?" Ashley asked.

"I am far from sure it would be wise for you to seek employment as a governess anywhere," Alcida told her.

"I concur," Lady Lancaster said. "Ashley would not be safe living in any household with a susceptible male." She gazed sternly at Ashley. "Masquerading as a songbird, you will have your own private home and a person wise in the ways of the theater to watch out for you. Not entirely safe, mayhap, but an improvement over the alternative."

"But Alcida, could I not simply go on the stage and sing with you in London?" Ashley asked.

Alcida and Lady Lancaster looked at one another. "It may come to that," Alcida admitted. "I believe we should give Lady Lancaster's plan a trial first, though. Whatever faults His Grace may prove to have, he is not tight-fisted. You could not hope to earn as much on the stage as he is offering. The amount is ridiculously elevated for a governess, so before we consider becoming a sister act, we shall see what he expects for his money."

Lady Lancaster nodded her agreement.

Ashley, outvoted, ceased to protest, though she remained uncertain the scheme was the best solution.

Three days later, posing as Ashley, Alcida set off for Humber's Harp after stopping by the Grahams' to say goodbye and collect her wardrobe. The masquerade went off without a hitch. She thought they seemed happy that Ashley had not perished with the measles but at the same time relieved that she was finally on her way to becoming Lady Clematis's governess.

The Reverend Mr. Mills had called earlier at the Dower House of Lancaster Hall to deliver Ashley's locket and inquire about her health. He, too, had not discerned the masquerade. Alcida had given the locket to Ashley and still wore her own, both sisters having reasoned that it would be perfectly safe.

Ashley herself was to remain with Lady Lancaster until the groom returned with the landau to drive her and Freddie to Alcida's small house in London.

Alcida could not but think the masquerade a great adventure. She had never lived anywhere except in the city, and like many Londoners who did not own large country estates, condemned any rural area as dull and backward. To her surprise, she found the freshness of Lincolnshire air to her liking. The rural countryside here, though somewhat bleak in comparison to the lushness of Kent, was pleasing to the eye. Buildings did not crowd one another, jostling for space. The sweep of the fields and marshes and even the stony wold fascinated her.

I believe, she thought in wonder, I might enjoy living here.

One problem remained. Since her education had been somewhat haphazard, she hadn't the slightest idea what she would teach Lady Clematis. Except to sing, perhaps. As the girl learned a new song, she could encourage her to illustrate the words with sketches. Beyond that, she had no real notion of what a governess did. Teach arithmetic? She was quite proficient with numbers.

Walks on the estate would be healthful, she decided, and she did know how to ride. Presumably the girl did, too, so that offered a time-consuming activity.

For the first time she wondered what Lady Clematis must be like, considering the strange gossip about her father. Secretive? Brash? Outgoing? Retiring? Soon she would know.

As for His Grace, she would have to bide her time to discover whether the local whisperings had any basis or not. Ashley had told her about the ghost of the beheaded first duke playing the harp at night. Alcida shook her head. She did not believe in ghosts.

"They do put the creatures in plays and such," her foster mother, Lucy Blayne, had been prone to say, "but I have never seen so much as one tiny little ghost in all my born days and likely never will."

Neither had Alcida, and she did not expect to see

any at Humber's Harp. She fell to speculating on what the duke looked like. Ashley had not described him to any great extent other than to comment on his darkness. Since gray hair had not been mentioned, he must be relatively young. Lady Lancaster characterized him as a recluse, and that agreed with her own tentative observation. She had never heard his name mentioned in London, so obviously he eschewed the city and the *haute ton.*

I am determined to enjoy this governess interlude, she told herself. 'Twill not last forever—two years at the most—and then Ashley and I can be together, as we were meant to be. It also provides me with a welcome vacation from the city and the importunate gentlemen who plague me with offers I do not wish to accept.

A momentary doubt ruffled her as to how her sister would cope with these constant and sometimes tempting offers. She shrugged it away. Between Ursula and Freddie, Ashley would be well enough shielded. True, her sister was an innocent, but she was not cork-witted. Ashley would be all right.

By contrast, Ashley was full of doubts. The nearer she came to London, the more apprehensive she grew. "How am I to perform in front of throngs of people?" she asked Freddie, having insisted he sit next to her in the landau rather than play the role of the footman. She desperately needed someone friendly to talk to.

Freddie shrugged. "Pretend they ain't there."

She frowned at him, but then, considering the idea, realized its merit. Had she not, in the privacy of the glen, pretended to be Queen of England, among other fanciful roles? If she could imagine herself alone in the glen, perhaps she could get through the song routines Alcida had taught her. Learning them had been wonderful fun, as well as easy.

"You are a natural at this, love," Alcida had assured her. "Your voice may be better suited for plaintive ballads than lively tunes, whereas mine is the opposite, but that is not a flaw. You will simply announce to the manager that you will be trying a new style of singing. Since I am well known for making changes in my routine—all successful, mind you—he will not so much as blink."

"Folks back 'ome liked your singing ever so much," Freddie told Ashley. "Stands to reason they will in London, folks being folks."

Maybe so, but London folks included lords and ladies who belonged to the *haute ton*. Although, come to think on it, she had sung for Squire Mitred's guests when she was younger and afterward, several of his London visitors had tried to make a pet of her, telling her how sweetly she sang and what a pretty little girl she was. Squire's wife had put a stop to that, whisking her away from the guests and sending her home.

"Wonder what Ursula be like," Freddie said. "Bound to be fierce, 'cause Miss Alcida calls her the Dragon Lady."

"*I'm* Miss Alcida," Ashley reminded him.

" 'Tis 'ard to keep that in me 'ead."

"You merely have to accustom yourself to thinking of me as my sister. Langdon seems to believe you can do anything you set your mind to."

Freddie stared at her. " 'E does? Mr. 'igh-'n-'mighty

Langdon? What do ye know about that? If 'e thinks so, maybe I can."

Maybe I can, too, Ashley told herself. I must, or all Lady Lancaster's careful plans will be for naught. Still, the two years stretching ahead of her seemed an age to be separated from the sister she had so recently found. Then again, Humber's Harp might prove too much for Alcida to cope with. If so, they would be together sooner.

"Lord Damon's gonna be set back on 'is 'heels, ain't 'e?" Freddie asked. " 'Cause now ye really are Alcida Blayne."

Startled, she realized there was a strong probability she and Lord Damon would meet in London because surely he would not give up his pursuit of the London songbird. 'Twould be a complete turnabout. He would not know she was actually Ashley Douglas—what sweet revenge. 'Twas her turn to humbug him. If he did not tumble to the masquerade. Still, she had gammoned him once, albeit unknowingly. Why not again?

Ashley smiled, savoring their meeting. Remembering Liam Gounod calling her a little yellow bird, her smile grew broader. Mr. Gounod would be far less of a threat to any woman's virtue than Lord Damon. And she was not in the slightest afraid of Liam. How exasperating Lord Damon would find it if Miss Blayne seemed to prefer his friend's company to his.

Concocting various ways to provoke Lord Damon reduced her apprehension, occupying her pleasantly for the remainder of the long journey. In the glen she may not have whistled him down the wind but she fully intended to in London.

Eight

Alcida arrived at Humber's Harp early in the afternoon. An elderly butler, so old he tottered rather than walked, advised her that his name was Hancock and informed her that she would meet His Grace and Lady Clematis at the evening meal. He then turned her over to the housekeeper, the equally ancient, though more spry, Mrs. Eldritch.

Mrs. Eldritch looked her up and down before producing a middle-aged maid named Betsy. "Show Miss Douglas to the Indian Room," she instructed the maid.

"Please to follow me, Miss," Betsy said, wending her way up the grand sweep of a magnificent curving staircase only dimly seen because of the gloom shrouding the mansion's interior. The dismal darkness quite matched the drive leading to the Hall, where large plane trees interspersed with yews met overhead to keep out the rays of the June-bright sun. There was also a moat, of all things, with water so dark one could almost believe monsters dwelt in its depths.

Yet Alcida's impression of the architecture of the house, with its impressive crenallated tower, tended to be favorable. Except, of course, for what appeared to be the intentional gloom inside and outside, where vastly overgrown shrubbery encroached on its stone exterior.

As Alcida followed Betsy up the stairs, she noted that the massive iron and brass chandelier in the Great Hall below held a full quota of fat white candles, none of which was lit. 'Tis almost as though the duke intends to intimidate visitors by plunging them into darkness, she thought with annoyance. She had been hoping to catch a glimpse of the haunted harp, rumored to be in the Great Hall, but the dimness below made it impossible to discern how the Hall was furnished.

Judging by what she'd experienced so far, Alcida did not expect to walk down well-lighted corridors when they reached the next floor, so she was prepared. Wings, presumably containing bedchambers, spread to either side of this floor's sitting hall where family portraits hung. At least Alcida assumed they were of family; it was difficult to see well enough even to be certain they were portraits of people.

Betsy turned to the right, walked past four doors, and threw the fifth open. "The Indian Room, Miss," she announced.

Naturally this room was no brighter than anything else at Humber's Hall. The servants were most efficient, however, because her two bags already had been brought up.

"If ye don't mind, Miss," Betsy said, "I'll unpack for ye."

"Wait!" Alcida cried. "I wish that you shall first throw open those red drapes and let the sun in."

Betsy slanted her a look that said plainer than

words that the new governess was already violating house custom. "If ye wish, Miss," Betsy replied reluctantly.

"I most fervently do so wish."

Once the Turkey red drapes had been pulled to either side of the windows and fastened back with gold cords, Alcida took her first good look at her surroundings. A massive painting of a many-armed, dark-skinned woman glared menacingly down at her from above the fireplace, whose tiles depicted fanciful serpents and other reptiles. The mantel was decorated along the edges with reliefs of hideously grinning monkeys.

No wallpaper graced the room. Above what appeared to be teakwood wainscoting, the walls were painted green. In one corner lurked what, for lack of any other word, Alcida could only think of as a triangular bed—made to fit into the corner. The brass headboard, also fitted cornerwise, boasted green metal vines creeping up the many brass rods between the two posts. She had no doubt that on close examination, she might find what were meant to be unpleasant surprises hidden among those metal vines.

Filmy paisley draperies were suspended from the tall headboard and attached to extending metal rods so that they could enclose the bed's occupant, if desired. Without taking in any more of the bizarre room, Alcida decided that if ever a bedchamber had been designed for intimidation followed by seduction, this one certainly was. Terrify the young lady with scary pictures and snakes and then take her to the haremlike bed and have your way with her while she was still reeling with shock.

She could not imagine Ashley in this room, but as for her, she found it an amusing challenge. His Grace would soon learn she was not easily intimidated—or seduced. As for the unusual bed, she might even enjoy sleeping in it. Alone.

Glancing at the rest of the room, she noticed the deep red background of the Turkish carpet had a design that reprised the coiled motif of the snakes and vines in varying shades of green relieved by off-white and black. The two lamps were composed of a bronze monkey apiece holding up bowls to be lit.

Uncomfortable-looking teakwood and gilt furniture was scattered here and there, and a leather gout stool in the form of a large turtle skulked beneath the windows.

Alcida looked at Betsy, who was watching her covertly, smiled, and said, "How charmingly different."

Betsy blinked and blurted, "Do ye like it, then?"

Alcida turned slowly around as though deliberately reviewing the room's contents again. "Not like, no," she said, "but I shall feel at home here because it reminds me of the excesses I have observed in—" She broke off barely in time, for she had been about to say "London."

Ashley had never been to London, and quite likely the duke was aware of this. She must guard her tongue, remembering at all times she was not Alcida; she was Ashley.

Alcida was hoping for information about those who lived at Humber's Harp, but Betsy did not volunteer another word as she placed the new governess's clothes in a massive teak and brass wardrobe, the one piece of furniture in the room that Alcida admired.

Reverting to direct questions, Alcida asked, "Has Lady Clematis had previous governesses?"

"No, Miss."

"Perhaps she attended a school?"

"No, Miss."

Confused, Alcida said, "But I understand she is eleven. Surely she must read and write."

"His Grace taught her hisself."

Prying information from Betsy was harder than coaxing an unresponsive audience to enthusiasm. She could but hope at least one of the other servants would prove to be more talkative.

For the most part, she had contented herself with her sister's rustic gowns, all but one with an unmodish high neckline. The green riding habit she had brought along, however, belonged to her, and it was in the very latest style. She wondered if Betsy had noticed the contrast, then shrugged. Betsy did not matter—Thomas Farrington, Eighth Duke of Roxton, was the person she had to get around in one way or another. And also, to some extent, his daughter, though an eleven-year-old, should be easier to fool than a thirty-some-year-old duke.

"What is Lady Clematis like?" she asked.

Betsy stopped folding her nightgown into a drawer and looked at her. A long moment passed before she said, "She's a lonely child."

Lonely. That had not been one of the words Alcida had come up with when she'd wondered about her new charge. She immediately felt sorry for the girl, telling herself if she was not able to teach Lady

Clematis very much of anything, at least she could try to be the girl's friend.

"She does ride?"

"Yes, Miss."

Alcida nodded, reassured. She would begin by riding with her charge, and while they were exercising the horses, learn more about the girl so she would have some idea of where to go from there.

She did not intend to worry about the duke unless he became a problem.

Betsy finished her task, mentioned that a bell would be rung to announce dinner, and left, shutting the door behind her. Almost immediately it unlatched and swung slightly open, remaining ajar.

"Is someone there?" Alcida asked.

There was no answer, nor did the door move either to or fro.

Shrugging away an uneasiness, Alcida decided to leave the door as it was. After all, if there were such things as ghosts, 'twas not likely a closed door or even a locked one would stop them from entering.

She had begun to putter about the room, marveling at the strange relics that had found a home in her bedchamber, when suddenly she felt she was being watched. Discarding the notion the watcher might be the duke—he would not be so surreptitious—she decided it must be the girl. Walking to the door, she opened it all the way. No one was there or in the hall, and yet she still felt the eyes.

Choosing boldness over reticence, she closed the door and announced, "I should like to meet you, Lady Clematis. Come out, come out, wherever you are." The last few words were borrowed from one of her stage songs, so she sang them.

One of the wainscoting panels slid open, startling her, and a thin, pale wraith of a girl ducked into the room. The panel slid closed behind her. Without looking at Alcida, she whispered, "I pray you will not be angry."

"Heavens, no," Alcida said. "I knew Humber's Harp would be an interesting diversion, although I admit I did not expect secret passageways. I find myself fascinated by your rather unorthodox entrance." She concealed her frisson of fear at the notion that secret passageways implied secret visitors. She had no desire to wake up some night and discover His Grace had crept into her bedchamber through that panel.

She smiled at Lady Clematis, whose hair was as pale a red as hers was dark, and, deciding to be as honest as possible under the circumstances, said, "I am Miss Ashley Douglas, here to teach you—at least, I hope I know enough to be able to teach you. You may prove to be more learned than I."

The girl's light blue eyes crinkled a bit, as though she were repressing a smile.

"Do you sing?" Alcida asked.

"Sometimes." Lady Clematis spoke so softly she could scarce be heard. "I like music."

"Then we shall get on famously, because I enjoy singing above all else and shall teach you every song I know. How about riding?"

The girl's face brightened. "Will you ride with me? Papa will not allow me to go without a groom, and I do not care for a groom trailing after me. You can, if you will, ride Ceres, she so badly needs exercise."

She stopped abruptly, as though fearing she'd said too much.

"We shall ride in the morning," Alcida assured her. "For now, if you still feel troubled about emerging from the wall of my room, you might, to make amends, teach me the secret of how the panel opens and closes."

Lady Clematis was not only willing, but eager. It seemed the panel closed by itself once opened from the inside. One could also open it by firmly pressing the fireplace tile which bore the picture of an extremely evil-looking hooded cobra.

"I learned about the passageways from a book in the library," Lady Clematis said. "There are peepholes inside, too, you know. I have never dared tell Papa—must you?"

"I do not see why," Alcida said. "The book is there for him to read, as you did, if he is interested."

"Papa worries about me overmuch, and I fear he would forbid me to use any of the passageways if he discovered I knew about them."

"He shall not hear about your escapades from me," Alcida vowed. "We shall have a secret between us—perhaps the first of many."

A giggle, quickly stifled, escaped the girl. "I did not know what you would be like," she said. "I have never had a governess before, you see. I feared you might be terribly strict."

"Never! Shall we share a second secret? I have not been a governess before and I am far from sure what to do. I intend to practice on you. We shall sing and ride and perhaps try a little sketching. Beyond that, we shall have to put our heads together and concoct a plan."

Lady Clematis giggled again, this time not bothering to stifle it. "I did not expect you would want me to enjoy myself."

"Whyever not? How can I enjoy myself if you are unhappy?"

"Oh, I am ever so glad you came here!"

"So am I." At least so far, Alcida added to herself, reminded that she had not yet met Lady Clematis's father.

"I really should go." The girl spoke with obvious reluctance.

"You may stay if you wish."

Lady Clematis shook her head. "If I am not downstairs, Papa is likely to come looking for me. I would rather keep our meeting a secret. The third one?"

Alcida smiled, liking the girl better every moment. "We shall have a bag full in no time. I pray you will come and collect me for dinner, though. I am certain I shall never find my way through the gloom to the dining room."

Lady Clematis gave her a puzzled look. "Gloom?"

Did not the child realize how ill-lit her house was? "I am accustomed to rather more light," Alcida said. "And, of course, I do not yet know my way about."

"If I cannot come, I shall be sure to send my abigail to direct you." She started to reach a hand toward Alcida, then drew it back as though fearing Alcida might not want to be touched.

Having none of that, Alcida grasped the girl's hand and pressed it before releasing her. "I hope we shall be friends," she said.

"I wish it with all my heart," Lady Clematis said fervently, exiting through the door which had come ajar once more.

Alcida examined the door but found no reason why it would not stay closed. There was a lock but no key, and no bolt on the inside, either. She gnawed on her lip as she decided what she could do. A movable piece of furniture placed in front of the door before she retired might not keep anyone out but would warn her if anyone tried to enter. As for the sliding panel, she would have to cobble something together to make a noise if the panel moved.

Her glance drifted to a wide, ornately decorated leather strip hung over a small writing desk. Attached to the strip were brass bells—"camel bells," she had heard them called. She nodded. The bells would hang elsewhere at night.

That evening, wearing the only fashionable gown Ashley owned, a blue silk, Alcida followed Lady Clematis down the staircase just as the dinner bell sounded. The candles in the massive chandelier were not lit. Instead, wall sconces provided flickering, inadequate illumination. As they passed through the Great Hall, Alcida paused momentarily beside a beautiful golden harp, uncovered, as though someone was about to sit on the gilded stool beside it and pluck the harp strings. Or did she mean some*thing?*

She shook her head and walked on. If and when music came from the harp, she was determined to believe human fingers made that music.

By the time they reached the dining room, Alcida

felt herself overwhelmed by the sheer size of the mansion. One could easily become lost here, she must be careful. When they entered the dining room, she was pleased to note that candelabra on a sideboard and on a server as well as on the table had all their candles lit. Apparently the duke wished to see what he was eating. As though her thought had evoked him, a man appeared from the shadows at the far end of the room, a man who could only be Thomas Farrington, Eighth Duke of Roxton.

"Promptness is an underrated virtue," he said in a deep voice. "I am pleased to find you possess it, Miss Douglas. Welcome to Humber's Harp."

She offered a polite curtsy and a "Thank you, sir," before looking him in the face. Her eyes widened. Ashley had given her no idea of how devilishly handsome he was. Eyes so dark as to appear black gazed appraisingly at her from an angled face crowned by a thick shock of black hair.

He was over six feet tall, broad-shouldered, and fit, wearing exquisitely tailored clothes that were slightly out of fashion. When he advanced toward her, she controlled her impulse to back away.

No man would intimidate her!

His gaze fixed on her face and she met the full force of those gleaming dark eyes without blinking but not without being affected. A strange tingling ran along her spine. She knew it was not fear, though she had to admit she could not be certain what had caused the tingling.

He reached for her unoffered hand, grasped it, and brought the back of her hand to his lips. This was not the first time a gentleman had kissed her hand, so why did warmth spread from the touch of his lips on her hand to diffuse throughout her body?

"I cannot tell you how pleased I am to have you here," he said, the deep tone of his voice reaching to the very marrow of her bones. "My daughter and I have been waiting most impatiently for your arrival. I trust you are recovered from your illness."

Gathering her wits, which seemed to have scattered at his touch, Alcida said, "I am quite well, sir."

"I see you have become acquainted with Clematis," he said.

"Yes, sir." What had happened to her that she could not do more than dumbly answer his observations?

"Papa, we should like to ride tomorrow morning, with your permission," Lady Clematis said.

"You do ride, then?" His tone indicated surprise.

"Adequately, I assure you." Thank heaven she was returning to some semblance of herself, instead of continuing to respond like a goose-witted ninny.

"You are more talented than I realized," he told her.

"I feel quite certain, sir, you have learned not to judge a book by its cover."

He offered her his arm to lead her to her chair at the table, murmuring, as his gaze rested at her neckline, "An attractive cover for most interesting contents."

She shot him a speaking glance. He was fast becoming much too forward. Placing her hand lightly on his sleeve so as to barely touch him, she allowed him to seat her at what would be his right. When he had seated his daughter to his left and dropped into his own chair at the head of the table, she said, "I trust we have your permission to ride in the morning."

"With one of the grooms attending, I see no reason why not."

With a sideways glance at her father to make certain he was not looking at her, Clematis made a brief moue at Alcida, indicating she had hoped not to be burdened with a groom. In truth, neither did Alcida, but she would offer no objections to His Grace's rules. Not yet.

"The dining room is especially cheerful with so many candles lit," she said, the first stroke in her campaign to attempt to reduce the gloom at the mansion. Actually, the room was so large that the far end remained shadowed because the light was concentrated on and near their end of the long table. Still, it was an improvement.

"Do you think so? I had not noticed." The duke did not seem interested in pursuing the subject.

"I believe Miss Douglas finds our house rather gloomy," Lady Clematis put in.

Her father blinked and tasted his soup before turning to Alcida to say with a certain finality, "I have grown accustomed to the dark."

If he'd thought to discourage her, he was in for a surprise. "You require darkness because your vision is afflicted, sir?" she asked, wearing her most innocent expression.

"There is nothing wrong with my eyesight!" His tone persuaded Alcida to leave well enough alone for the moment.

"I wish to tell you how grateful I am that you have settled me into the Indian Room," she ventured after a few spoonfuls of not quite warm-enough turtle soup. She would deal with the too-cool soup at another time. "I am charmed by the furnishings."

He eyed her dubiously. "Charmed, are you?"

She widened her eyes, hoping she was not overacting the part of the rustic maiden. "Who would not be fascinated by such unique decorating?"

"Miss Douglas likes to sing and plans to teach me new songs," Lady Clematis said, evidently used to conversing with her father at the dinner table.

"I have heard her sing," he said.

Alcida's breath quickened in alarm. She had supposed he so rarely came to the city that there would be no danger he would recognize her as the London songbird. Had he so quickly penetrated her masquerade?

"At a midsummer fair near Louth, I believe it was," he continued.

Alcida chided herself for not immediately recalling that her sister had often been asked to sing at fairs and such. She was safe. He had not known Ashley well enough to realize he was stuck with a ringer.

"Your voice is lovely," he told her. "Truly memorable."

Though she understood he was complimenting Ashley, she still felt pleased. "You are too kind," she murmured.

"In this case, I speak the truth. As you will discover, I am not kind . . . rather the opposite."

Quashing her temptation to cry sarcastically, "Ooh, you frighten me, you do," she made no comment. They were well into the third course when she realized how much she was enjoying holding her own with the duke. He must realize by now that he had incorrectly assessed Ashley Douglas and that she was going to prove more of a challenge than he had believed.

She quite looked forward to their next meeting. Which, in the event, turned out to be sooner than she had expected.

With her alarms in place, she passed a restful night and woke early to a tapping at the door. Hastily rising, she hurried to return the small table she'd placed in front of the door to its proper place. The door immediately swung ajar of its own accord. Alcida peered through the opening, and seeing a young maid standing in the corridor, swung the door open, inviting her inside.

The maid entered, curtsied, and said, "I be Janet, Miss. Lady Clematis says I'm to help ye. Brought ye yer morning tea, I did."

Alcida had not expected to have a personal maid. From what Lady Lancaster had told her, governesses inhabited an uncertain place somewhere between a servant and a guest. While often asked to dine with the family, they were not waited on by the servants as a guest would be.

"How nice, Janet," she said. "I shall thank Lady Clematis for her thoughtfulness."

"I ain't been here long," Janet added. "Ain't never been a lady's maid afore, neither."

"Since I have never been a governess before, we should rub along very well."

"Do ye want I should lay out yer clothes, Miss?" Janet asked.

"The green riding habit, if you please."

" 'Tis ever so pretty," Janet remarked, as she removed the habit from the wardrobe, her fingers stroking the soft twill.

The habit had cost a pretty penny, more than Alcida should have spent, but 'twas important for a lady in the public eye to keep up with the fashions and dress well. She had never imagined she would be wearing the habit outside of London. Who could have predicted the chain of events that had led her to Humber's Harp?

How, she wondered, was her sister faring in London, if she had arrived there as yet? The city itself might prove overwhelming at first, but Ashley, she thought, would do fine once she had her first performance behind her. Her sister, though a country maiden, was neither timid nor hen-witted, and she was quick to learn. With Ursula's help, she should have few problems.

How much easier it was to dress with Janet's assistance rather than to struggle on her own. Alcida blessed Lady Clematis for thinking of her. New maid or not, Janet was proving proficient. Only when it came to her hair did the girl back off, shaking her head. "Never done no lady's hair, Miss. Might make a mess of it,"

"I shall teach you. Luckily, mine is easy to do, since it curls by itself quite naturally. You shan't have a bit of trouble. Here, take this brush."

Janet's first tentative brushstrokes soon grew more skilled. When she finished, under guidance, Alcida's hair curled riotously over her head in the way she favored.

" 'Tis a shame to fit that riding hat over your hair,

Miss," Janet observed. "Never afore seen such a pretty color of red. Don't look hardly real."

Alcida smiled at her. "I was born with it. Thank you for helping me, Janet." She rose from the vanity stool, adjusted her riding hat into place, then, carrying her gloves, left her bedchamber, having arranged to meet Lady Clematis at the stables. As she descended into the gloom of the Great Hall, she saw a dim figure below. By the time she neared the bottom of the stairs, she had recognized the duke, but since he did not speak, neither did she, though her heart began to hammer in a most annoying fashion.

"Good morning, Miss Douglas," he said, when she came face to face with him in the Hall. "My daughter has gone on ahead. I remained behind to escort you to the stables."

"How kind, sir," she said, eyeing his riding habit. "Are we to be honored with your presence on our morning ride?"

Without warning, he grasped her still ungloved hand. His hand was likewise bare. At the contact of flesh against flesh, Alcida's insides began to quiver while a tingling warmth invaded her. She tried to tug her hand away but he refused to release it.

"Why is it," he asked, "that innocent though your words are, I sense you are funning me?"

Alcida fought to regain her equilibrium. Why must his touch affect her in such a disquieting fashion? "I am sure I do not know what you mean, sir."

"But you do, my dear, you know very well. You are not at all the young lady I expected, Miss Douglas."

She finally succeeded in wresting her hand from his and hurriedly began to put on her gloves, wondering what she had done to make him suspect she was not a country maiden. At least he still believed she was Ashley.

Giving him her best earnest gaze, she said, "The world is a perilous place for young ladies, sir. We learn early to tread warily among the snares and devices cast into our path."

He stepped to the front door and opened it, lightening the Hall's darkness. As he gestured for her to precede him, he asked, "Which is it you suspect me of casting?"

She slanted him a glance as she passed, aware it was unwise to flirt with him, but enjoying the risk. "I am certain you are far too clever to resort to the obvious."

After closing the door, he offered her his arm. Again, she tried to touch it as lightly as possible. "You are mistaken, Miss Douglas," he said. "I am not clever."

"Oh?"

"Call me determined and you will be far closer to the mark."

"Determined, sir?"

He nodded. "What I go after, I get, Miss Douglas. Always. Make no mistake about it."

A shiver of mixed apprehension and anticipation ran along her spine. He had no idea what kind of an opponent he faced this time; she would do her utmost to defeat him. Unfortunately, her confidence in winning had been shaken by what happened to her when he touched her. No man had ever before addled her wits with a mere clasp of his hand.

Apparently she must conquer herself before she could be sure of conquering him.

Nine

"I cannot, there is no use in trying. I simply cannot do it, I am in a terrible fidget." Wringing her hands, Ashley stared into the vanity mirror at Ursula's face, in her misery hardly seeing the square jaw and blue eyes or the gray hair that peeked from under a lacy cap. "I will admit I have sung to people before, but I was not on a London stage with the *haute ton* as my audience. I declare, I feel quite ill."

"Nonsense." Ursula's voice, as usual, was calm. "Everyone who performs suffers what is known as stage fright. No more than that ails you. Once you go out on the stage and sing a few notes, you will recover."

"Alcida is so much more talented than I. I am convinced they will sense the difference immediately."

"I remember your sister's first appearance alone on the stage," Ursula said. "She suffered from stage fright, too."

Ashley stared at her. "Alcida was afraid? She seems so assured and capable."

"Capable she is, but nevertheless, she has had her moments of insisting she could not possibly perform. Yet she did—as you will do. Try to remember how closely you resemble your sister and do consider that no one in London except for Freddie and me is aware Alcida has a twin sister. They are sure to believe you are she and will not pay any attention to a slight difference in performance, if indeed there should be one."

Ashley bit her lip. "What you say is true, yet I continue to shiver in my slippers. I dislike above all believing that I am a coward."

"Then don't be one." Ursula leaned forward and adjusted the saucy little green hat decorated with roses that sat atop Ashley's short auburn curls, tipping it slightly forward.

Ashley was still not accustomed to her shorter hair, cut the day before she'd left Lincolnshire so as to match the length of Alcida's. Yet she had to agree that the short curls were attractive and easy to care for, not to mention being in the first stare of fashion.

Glancing down at the pomona green silk gown she wore—one of Alcida's—she told herself that Mrs. Graham would have a case of the vapors if she saw how low the neckline was. She herself adored the dress, the most attractive she had ever worn. Her very own heart locket nestled at her throat and she reached to touch it, hoping the feel of the cool gold would give her confidence.

"Because, like Alcida, you are such a pretty girl," Ursula said, "they come to see you as well as to hear you sing. No one can possibly know you are not Alcida tonight since you are the exact image of her. I have listened to you, and your voice is so similar I swear if I closed my eyes I could believe I heard Alcida singing. Nothing will go wrong tonight, you have my word on it."

Ashley sighed. "I realize I must appear. I only wish I were not terrified."

A tap at the door announced Freddie's arrival in his new green footman's uniform. At her "Enter," he bounced in only to stop short, goggling at her. "Rats and mice!" he cried. "If ye ain't smashing."

"Thank you." Ashley pushed the words through her tight throat. "I think you make a truly handsome footman yourself. Does he not, Ursula? Look how well the green goes with his red hair."

He grinned at them both, swaggering a bit. "If Sandy from the 'Arp 'n' Whistle saw me now, 'e wouldn't trust 'is own eyes, 'e wouldn't."

The mention of the Inn reminded her of poor Alcida, stranded at Humber's Harp while she was here enjoying the sights of London. Or at least, she had been, until the time had come for this first stage appearance.

"I do hope my sister is not under duress," she said.

"Alcida is well able to shift for herself," Ursula assured her. "She has been doing so for many years. I will hazard a guess that at this very moment she is worrying about you rather than herself."

Freddie clicked his heels together. Standing stiff and straight, he intoned, "Yer carriage awaits, Miss."

Smiling at his notion of the proper behavior for a footman, Ashley gave herself one last look in the mirror for reassurance. Everything was as perfect as Ursula could make it. The rest depended on her. "Say a prayer for me, Alcida," she murmured, as she descended the front steps, "and I shall say one for you."

The bustle at the Haymarket—carriages arriving with ladies and gentlemen alighting to enter the thea-

ter—heightened her apprehension until she was
aquiver with dread. This will not do, she warned herself, as she entered by a side door with Freddie and
Ursula. I must conquer this fear here and now, or I
shan't be able to so much as walk onto the stage.

What was it Liam Gounod had called her—or
rather, called Alcida, because that was who he had
believed she was. *A little yellow bird from the Isles.* She
paused and closed her eyes momentarily, trying to
imagine herself as a yellow bird, able to fly away when-
ever she wished.

"Miss!" Freddie exclaimed. "Miss Ash—Alcida. I
seen 'im, I did. E's come to 'ear ye sing."

Forcing her attention to Freddie, Ashley asked
"Whom did you see?"

"Lord Damon, that's 'oo."

Ashley had not considered that he might be present at her Haymarket debut. He would see her fail.
A wave of sheer panic swept over her, then receded
leaving numbness in its wake. As Ursula fussed over
her, rearranging a curl here and a fold of cloth there
the heat of Ashley's annoyance at Lord Damon
gradually melted the numbness. She would *not* fail.

" 'Is friend's with 'im," Freddie reported, on his
return from peeping at the audience through a spy
hole in the stage curtain.

"Mr. Gounod?"

Freddie nodded.

Chance favors me rather than working against me
Ashley decided. Liam Gounod does not scare me. I
I can bring myself to imagine the audience is composed of others such as Mr. Gounod, rather than a
multitude of Lord Damons sitting in judgment, per

haps I can convince myself I am akin to the little yellow bird Liam called me, and, like the bird, sing because I wish to sing.

Alcida had told her that theater audiences, being accustomed to plays, enjoyed having her arrange her songs to tell a story, which was what Ashley planned to do. She had strung her music together to create a tale of love found, betrayed, and lost, closing with the repentant lover returning and entreating to be forgiven.

Accordingly, she had chosen "The Lass with the Delicate Air" for the first song and "My Love Will Ne'er Forsake Me" at the end, to celebrate the lovers' reunion.

When the time came, in a daze, she stepped from the wings onto the stage. Though she had been told the backdrop for her performance was a forest glade, she was not aware of the backdrop nor any of her surroundings. The applause when she came into view of the audience took her aback. She had not sung one note and they were already clapping.

At the same time, their obvious approval gave her confidence. I am Alcida Blayne, she reminded herself, and I will behave the way she would. She faced them square on, smiling and blowing kisses, before launching into her beginning song.

By the time she reached the betrayal song, she was starting to enjoy herself. *"Black,"* she sang, *"is the color of my true love's hair . . ."* Her gaze, flitting over the audience, suddenly held as she recognized Lord Damon. To her credit, despite her pounding heart she did not stumble, continuing on to describe in song the lover whose heart was as black as his hair.

But time and again she glanced in his direction, unable to desist.

As Freddie had said, he was with Mr. Gounod; both were watching her with rapt attention. Neither man appeared to be accompanied by a female companion. Why this should please her was beyond her comprehension. Lord Damon was nothing to her, nothing at all.

She finished her last song and curtsied to the audience. As she started to rise, a pink rose dropped in front of her, thrown, she knew, from someone out front. She reached for the rose, making the bold gesture of thrusting it into her décolletage as she straightened. Other flowers, some in bouquets, followed the first until she was ankle deep in posies.

Overwhelmed by the response to her singing, Ashley blew kisses once again to the audience before retiring from the stage. She was still wearing the pink rose when, caped and gloved against the night's coolness, she emerged with Ursula from the side door, not remaining to view the skit that followed her singing. Freddie had seen to it that her hired hackney was waiting at the side door.

As she approached the hack, Lord Damon stepped out of the shadows and intercepted her path. He bowed and said, "I don't believe we have been introduced, Miss Blayne."

"That is true, sir," she said, amazed at the even tone of her voice when her heart was fluttering as though the little bird she had pretended to be was trapped within his grasp.

"I am Lord Damon," he said, "and I felt I must

tell you how charmed I was by your singing and the story concealed within your choice of songs."

"Thank you, sir." She tried to move ahead, and as she did so, stepped on a loose stone in the street. Her subsequent loss of balance caused her to throw out her arms to right herself. In doing so, her tight grip on her green velvet cape loosened and it fell open.

He smiled. "I see you are wearing my rose."

"I did not know who threw the rose," she told him.

"You have it nestled in such an enticing spot that I would gladly change places with the rose, were such a thing possible."

Ignoring his words because they were too impudent to acknowledge, she said, "I believe you are blocking the path to my hack, sir. Pray let me pass."

"Not until you agree to meet me in the park on the morrow."

"If you are referring to Rotten Row, I don't go there regularly, therefore I doubt we shall meet. And we have yet to be properly introduced."

"I will see to it that we are."

"By Lady Jersey, of course." Alcida had taught her enough about the *ton* so that she knew the names of some of the women who could make or break a young lady who wished to find a husband among the gentlemen of the *ton*.

He shrugged. "If you like."

She had spoken in jest, Alcida having stressed the difficulty of even being noticed by these women of the first order, much less acknowledged. "Lady Jersey, for example," she'd said, "would simply not see girls like us even if we committed the grave *faux pas* of sitting in her lap."

If Lord Damon was funning her, as he must be, she would set a trap for him. "I shall hold you to your promise, sir," she said pertly.

"As I shall hold you to yours."

She had made no promise and was about to say so when Liam Gounod appeared at Lord Damon's elbow. "Sly fox," Mr. Gounod accused his friend. "Slipping off when my back was turned. Knew where I'd find you, though." He bowed his head to Alcida. "Good evening, Miss Blayne." He nudged Lord Damon. "I should like above all to meet this beautiful songbird."

"So should I," Lord Damon retaliated. "But she requires an introduction by Lady Jersey before she will deign to notice us."

Mr. Gounod blinked, evidently at a loss for words. But not for long. "Dead ringer for the rustic maiden, ain't she? No wonder you were fooled."

"We." Lord Damon bit off the word.

"Pray allow me to pass, gentlemen," Ashley said, not relishing the turn of the conversation.

"Excuse me, gentlemen," Ursula said, advancing toward them. "Miss Blayne must not be out in the evening air after singing. Her throat will suffer and in the event we shall all be sorry. Do not, I pray, block her path."

Lord Damon inclined his head. "Until the morrow," he said. With a firm grip on Liam Gounod's arm, he turned away and the two men disappeared into the shadows.

"The morrow?" Ursula repeated, when they were seated inside the hack.

"He asked me to meet him at the park," Ashley confessed. "I did not agree. He claims he will have Lady Jersey introduce him to me properly, but I cannot believe such a rig."

"I realize you met him when he mistook you for Alcida," Ursula said. "You may or may not have enjoyed his company at that meeting, but I must warn you, he is considered a rake."

"I deduced that at the time and he has made it abundantly clear now. I shall not become another of his victims."

"Do not underestimate him," Ursula said. "I perceive he has intrigued you and I would hazard you will, after all, decide to meet him tomorrow. 'Tis not impossible you shall find he has somehow cozened Lady Jersey into making the introduction. He will then come to call."

"If this comes to pass, and I am not admitting that it will, I shall insist on Mr. Gounod's accompanying him. I quite like Liam Gounod."

Ursula's soft murmur of agreement managed to convey that she had heard Ashley's words but did not necessarily believe them.

" 'Tis of no consequence, in any case," Ashley said, abruptly changing the subject to a topic she told herself was of much more importance. "You have been proved right, Ursula. Once I began singing, my fears floated away like leaves before the wind. And nobody knew I was not—" She paused, mindful of the hired coachman who probably could not hear what she said. Still, it was well not to take any chances.

"Ye sang like an angel," Freddie said. "Always did think so."

"You are a loyal friend," She told him, feeling on top of the world. She had succeeded not only in making the audience believe she was Alcida; she had pleased them as well. Even Lord Damon had complimented her—though it was entirely possible he'd had his own reasons.

She had absolutely no intention of meeting him on the morrow.

At midafternoon, Ashley came down the stairs to be greeted by Ursula at the bottom. After looking her up and down, Ursula said, "Alcida took her new habit with her and did not send it back with you. Still, her last year's blue one you're wearing is modish enough and shows little wear."

Ashley had already discovered Ursula would not allow her to leave the premises unless she looked to be all the crack. "You cannot be in the public eye and dress unfashionably," Ursula had insisted. "Your sister learned this fact early and took pains to be always well turned out."

Ashley could not help but wonder what Ursula would say if she saw Alcida in some of the high-necked drab governess gowns made for Humber's Harp. They were not so much out of fashion as they were Mrs. Graham's overly modest idea of what should be in the mode for unmarried young ladies.

How was poor Alcida coping with His Grace? Ursula had warned of Lord Damon's reputation as a rake, but, Ashley decided, rake or not, Lord Damon would be a piece of cake compared to Thomas Farrington, Eighth Duke of Roxton.

"I felt in my bones you would ride this afternoon," Ursula said. " 'Tis a harmless enough diversion for young ladies if they keep their minds on the horse. 'Tis a shame we don't own a carriage, but you should have no difficulty with Mal. He is amiable except for that one habit."

Mal, Ashley knew, was her sister's chestnut gelding, named for the French word for bad because, though otherwise gentle, he would not tolerate anything with feathers near him. She had introduced herself to Mal, bribing him with sugar lumps in the hope he would be more favorably disposed toward a person who fed him sweets. She had not yet ventured to ride him.

In truth, she had not ridden overmuch at home. The Grahams owned no horse accustomed to a side-saddle and Mrs. Graham would not hear of her riding astride. On occasion she had been invited to ride Mrs. Mills's horse, and that had been her only proper experience. She could not very well count the times at home that, with Freddie's connivance, she had sneaked rides astride.

Still, she was comfortable around horses and felt she could manage Mal, even though she must ride sidesaddle.

"I shall have no difficulty keeping my mind on my horse," she assured Ursula. "I would not trouble to venture to Hyde Park were it not that I am curious to meet Lady Jersey. If that does not come to pass, I shall enjoy putting Lord Damon down for his failure to produce her. He is far too high in the instep."

"You are certain of your direction?"

"I believe so. In any case, Freddie will be with me and he is already as familiar with the streets of London as he is with the lanes and byways of Lincolnshire."

"He is indeed a treasure. I am attempting to teach him the proper way of speech as well as his letters. Learning to read comes easy for him, but changing his mode of speech promises to be difficult."

"I helped him learn his numbers a few years ago," Ashley said. "Mrs. Graham put a stop to it when she found out. She felt it was a waste of my time and his, for she did not believe stableboys needed to learn to add and to subtract, much less multiply and divide."

"I can understand her feeling, even though I don't share it," Ursula said, "because work on a farm is never done. I escaped from one and fled to London with a traveling troupe when I was very young, and I have never regretted doing so." Though she looked at a watercolor of a mountain tarn on the entry wall, Ashley thought she must be seeing the past instead.

"I have had marvelous adventures, I have worked with great actors, I have loved and lost, and I would not change one moment of my life in the theater. Alcida's foster mother was my best friend; I consider it a privilege to be with the child she raised." Ursula turned to Ashley and smiled. "Now here *you* are, adding another interesting page to my life story."

"My sister has told me how much she depends on you," Ashley said. "I know I would be at sixes and sevens without your help and companionship."

"Since I am not accompanying you on your ride," Ursula said, "I urge you to be wary. Gentlemen of

he *ton,* with no exceptions, consider theater people
o be fair sport. I pray you shall keep in mind that
ou are not Ashley but Alcida and do all you can to
guard her reputation, as I am sure she is guarding
ours."

Ursula's cautionary words dampened Ashley's spir-
ts somewhat as she set off with Freddie, who was rid-
ng a borrowed pony. Though it would have been
more appropriate to drive to the park in a rig of some
sort, it would not do to appear in a rented one and
Alcida could not afford to keep both a riding horse
and a carriage horse. Nor had she the room on her
small property. So 'twas Mal or nothing.

Perched somewhat uneasily on the saddle at first,
Ashley grew more comfortable as they made their way
toward the park. Luckily, Alcida's house was not in
the heart of the city, for she would not have dared
o attempt the crowded streets. Ashley was not yet
aware of which were the fashionable residential sec-
tions of London, but she realized her sister's estab-
ishment was not in any of them, though the
surrounding area was pleasant enough—somewhat
rural, in fact.

She started when a pig ran across the road in front
of them, but Mal trotted on calmly, ignoring the animal.

"Like 'ome, almost," Freddie observed. " 'Cepting
t ain't, never mind them cows in the field over
here."

Ashley smiled vaguely, her thoughts already at the
park, rehearsing what she would say when she came
face to face with Lord Damon. Or should she say
nothing? Perhaps pretending he didn't exist was the

best choice. At least until he produced Lady Jersey
If he did. From what she had heard, she did not image Lady Jersey was as amiable as his aunt. Lady Lancaster went out of her way to help even ordinary
people, while Lady Jersey condescended to notice
only a select few, whom she might or might not help

"What yer gonna sing tonight?" Freddie asked.

"Seafaring songs," she replied absently.

"Maybe sometime ye'll sing about the fox 'n' the
'are."

"The fox and the hare?" she echoed. "I don't believe I know that one."

" 'Ere's the tune." Freddie began to whistle a
spritely air that caught Ashley's fancy.

"What are the words?" she asked.

He sang them in a high boy's voice that surprised
her with its clarity. The words told of an amusing
contest between the fox and the hare to see which
could outwit the other, but what happened was that
they succeeded only in outwitting themselves.

" 'Tis charming," she told him. "So is your voice."

His face was red as his hair. "Aw, 'tain't nothing
much."

"You have a very good voice," she insisted. "I can't
think why we never sang together back home."

"Master told me not to sing. Said it made the 'orses
restless."

The streets were rapidly becoming crowded as
every type of carriage, plus gentlemen on horseback,
converged on Hyde Park. Ashley was conscious of being surveyed by lady and gentleman alike. "Oh, dear,"
she said to Freddie, "I do believe I am the only

woman who is not seated in a carriage. Have I committed a *faux pas*?"

Before he could answer, a frantic squawking drew their attention to a chicken that had strayed into the road and was desperately endeavoring to avoid wheels and hooves. "She will be killed!" Ashley cried, trying to edge Mal closer to the side of the road so she might dismount and try to rescue the poor bird.

Ursula's warning about the horse's one peculiarity did not enter her mind until the chicken, still squawking loudly and shedding feathers, fluttered up directly in front of Mal. The horse emitted a terrified squeal, rose onto his hind legs, then came down and bolted off the road, galloping madly across a field as though being chased by the hounds of hell.

Though Ashley had managed not only to stay in the saddle but to keep hold of the reins, she had absolutely no control over the frightened animal. Trees and bushes flashed past in a blur of greenery. The rush of wind took her breath away and she could not tell whether the pounding she heard was her heart or the horse's hooves or both. She swayed to and fro, expecting at any minute to lose her balance and tumble onto the ground.

Suddenly another horse and rider loomed up on her right. She had barely enough time to think that it could not possibly be Freddie on his pony before the rider shouted, "Let go of the reins!"

Desperate, Ashley obeyed. A moment later the rider edged his horse closer, and the next she knew, strong arms jerked her up and out of the saddle, pulling her onto the other horse. She clung to her rescuer, burying her face in his shoulder.

His horse's pace gradually slowed, and his voice
calm and resonant, spoke soothingly to the animal
"Go easy, Monty, there's a good lad. Easy now, easy."

I know that voice, Ashley thought dazedly. When
the horse came to a stop, she pulled away and looked
up into the face of her rescuer.

"Lord Damon!" She gasped.

Ten

Lady Clematis beamed with delight at her father's presence as they began their morning ride. "You must show Miss Douglas everything," she told him. "The grotto, the abbey ruins, the pond in Gypsy Grove, the—"

"May I remind you that we are setting off on an hour's ride, Clematis." His reproof was indulgently gentle. "While the grotto and the ruins are reasonably close together, the pond is at the other end of the estate. We should be riding until midday."

"Oh, all right—the ruins and the grotto, then."

"I quite look forward to viewing the abbey ruins," Alcida said. "I have heard people speak of visiting Greece and seeing what remains of the ancient temples there. Some claim to have actually felt the presence of the old Greek gods."

"Do you believe in old gods?" the duke asked her.

"Since I have never yet felt myself in the presence of any, my reply must remain in abeyance until I visit Greece. Because I am not likely to do so in the foreseeable future, you may never have your answer, sir."

"Ably put, Miss Douglas. Or perhaps I should say *touché*, for again I have the distinct sensation that we are fencing."

"I fear fencing is not one of my accomplishments."

"I hope not," Lady Clematis put in. "I should not care to have you teach me swordplay of any kind for I always fall into a swoon at the sight of blood. Even the tiniest drop."

"Perhaps you will enjoy the grotto also," the duke said to Alcida, "since you find your bedchamber so compatible."

"Oh, do you raise snakes in the grotto, sir?" she asked, donning her most innocent expression.

He smiled one-sidedly. "Not on purpose. But of course, snakes do eat frogs, and frogs congregate where there is water. The grotto *is* damp."

"And green and slimy." Lady Clematis spoke with enthusiasm. " 'Tis ever so scary, Miss Douglas. And Papa forgot to tell you about the abbey's ghost."

"A ghost in the abbey, sir?" She longed to ask if the house also harbored a specter, but did not quite dare. "One of the monks?"

"Actually, the ghost is a woman. Or so they tell me. I have not had the doubtful pleasure of meeting her."

"She wears a flowing white robe and her long hair falls past her waist," Lady Clematis volunteered. "She floats about, wailing on nights when there is a full moon. I do wish I could see her just once."

Wasn't that rather an unhealthy wish for a young girl? Alcida wondered. Unusual, anyway . . .

As they rode across fallow fields and through clumps of trees, His Grace pointed out various sites as well as naming each bird they encountered. But when Alcida asked him about a pretty pink flower, he confessed he did not know what it was called.

"If your library contains books on wildflowers," Alcida said, "Lady Clematis and I shall collect and press those that grow on the estate, identifying them as we go along."

"A worthy project," he said. "No doubt the library has at least one book on any subject you can mention." Was there a touch of boredom in his tone? Alcida wasn't sure.

She hoped he was not laboring under the delusion that she had chosen the project to impress him. On the other hand, she could hardly admit that she had grasped eagerly at the opportunity because in this way both she and Lady Clematis could learn at the same time, while she would appear to be teaching her charge.

"I should like that," Lady Clematis said. "Perhaps we can sketch the flowers, too, and make up little songs about them."

Between the pair of them, 'twas easy to tell who was the natural teacher and who was not, Alcida thought wryly. "A wonderful idea," she said, evoking a shy smile from the girl.

When they were leaving the stables, Alcida had contrived to see that Lady Clematis rode between her and the duke, but as they neared the grotto, he urged his horse ahead, then made a half circle on his return, which placed him next to her. To conceal her frisson of excitement at his nearness, she leaned forward to stroke the neck of her bay mare.

"What a beautiful animal," she said.

"Beauty deserves beauty," he told her.

Flustered, she turned to Lady Clematis, saying, "I believe you mentioned her name yesterday, but alas, I have forgotten. Did it begin with a C?"

To her surprise, an alarmed expression flitted across the girl's face. "No, no," she said hastily. "My mare is Electra, Papa has Zeus, and you are riding Hebe."

"Hebe was chosen especially for you," the duke put in.

"I believe she was handmaiden to the gods," Alcida said, recalling that she had once had the role of Hebe when acting in a tableau with her foster mother. "I think the mare is lovely, but I must add that I do not see myself as anyone's handmaiden."

He raised one eyebrow. "No? Is not that a role most women undertake at some time in their lives?"

"As an orphan, sir, I did not have a father to play handmaiden to, should he have required it. And since I have no plans to marry, I do not anticipate having the role forced on me at any time soon."

"Forced on you? Shame, Miss Douglas. Women find it a privilege to cater to their husbands."

She gave him a level look. "Do they indeed, sir? We must be observing from different points of view."

He chuckled. "You need not worry. I promise I shall not attempt to coerce you into becoming my handmaiden."

"What *are* you talking about, Papa? Miss Douglas is my governess, not a maidservant."

He glanced at his daughter. "Quite right, my dear. I am merely funning her."

"I wish you shall stop, please," Lady Clematis said. "I am certain she would much rather hear about the grotto than be teased."

"I am not so sure you are right," he said, "but I promise to behave."

The grotto, a creation of the Third Duke of Roxton, proved to be as dank as His Grace had predicted, and with gargoyles grinning evilly from the mossy stone walls, almost as scary as Lady Clematis had claimed. The stone monsters disturbed Alcida far more than the reptilian replicas in her bedroom. Though she was not overfond of snakes. At least they had the virtue of being living creatures, while the gargoyles were naught but fanciful, ugly monsters.

"I sense you do not care for the grotto," the duke said. "Perhaps you are worried about a snake appearing."

"No, sir, I am not. But I cannot bring myself to admire the grotto. This place confirms my belief your ancestors must have had a propensity for gloominess."

"Gloominess? Why would you think that?" He seemed honestly puzzled.

In for a groat, in for a guinea, she told herself. "Your house, sir, is dark. Outside, greenery masks the sun, not allowing entry, and inside there is insufficient illumination." Aware she had been far too bold, she held her breath while waiting for his response.

"I had not noticed such a deficit." His tone rang with finality, convincing her that he tolerated criticism poorly and that she had best take heed.

Turning away from him, she trailed after Lady Clematis, who was climbing the stone steps leading up from the cavelike grotto to where they had left the horses. The duke seemed inclined to linger in the dank gloom.

When she reached the top, Lady Clematis drew her aside and saw in a low tone, "Please don't mention to Papa that I suggested you ride Ceres, for he is sure to be unhappy with me if you do."

Ceres. The name of the horse the girl had told her she would be riding. Curious, she would have asked why, but the scrape of boots on the stone warned the duke was about to join them.

"Our fourth secret," Alcida agreed, eliciting a wan smile from Lady Clematis.

The three of them remounted and rode on. As the duke had mentioned, the abbey ruins were not far off. Time, fire, and the depredations of long-ago looters had left only one wall standing. There was no roof at all, though here and there the remnants of chimneys poked above the rubble. The pleasantly pungent smell of herbs permeated the area, leading Alcida to comment on the amazing survival of garden plants in the most adverse of circumstances.

Lady Clematis perched atop a squared-off stone that had once formed part of the foundation and announced that she was going to keep watch for the ghost. " 'Tis not dark, but I never get to come here at night," she said. "I should think that ghosts would become bored, appearing at the same hour all the time, maybe she will change her pattern."

Before Alcida could offer to join her, the duke took her hand, tucked it under his arm, and said, "Miss Douglas and I will view the ruins while I bore her with the abbey's history. Be sure to call us if you spot the ghost."

"I shall. And would you not be surprised if I did, Papa?"

"Astounded."

As they wandered off, Alcida tried to calm her fluttering heart. Why was she so affected by him? 'Twas not as though she had not walked beside a man before. Never before, though, had any man made her breath catch when he'd touched her.

Determined to keep him from realizing her weakness, she searched for an innocuous topic, finally saying, "How fine the day. June is a wonderful month."

He smiled at her, a warm, intimate smile that turned her bones to jelly. "I don't know when I've enjoyed a morning ride more."

She couldn't decide whether to pull away from him or not. If she did, she could breathe easier, but on the other hand, since the ground was rough and rubble-strewn, in taking her arm, he had offered no more than common courtesy. It would be rude not to accept his help.

"Were you not intending to recite to me the abbey's history?" She said.

"No. Neither you nor I should enjoy such a recital in the slightest. Let us instead appreciate the warmth of the day and the pleasure of the company."

Which she was already appreciating far too much. Maybe she should be frightened of him, but she was not. What did make her apprehensive was herself. If one kept one's head, gentlemen could be discouraged without too much difficulty in whatever amorous pursuit they had in mind. But when one's head was dizzy with a man's touch and his nearness, one might find oneself in trouble.

"Actually, I am rather interested in old abbeys," she said, not quite truthfully.

"Are you indeed? Very well, then." As he spoke, he whisked her into what amounted to a roofless tunnel higher than their heads. "From what I can piece together, this led to the chapel. Up ahead the passage is blocked, and of course the chapel no longer exists. So we cannot go all the way." He slowed, stopping and leaned toward her, murmuring, "Perhaps this is far enough."

Alarmed by her urge to raise her face to his, Alcida pulled free of him. In doing so, she stepped onto a piece of rubble and lost her balance.

"Watch out!" He reached for her, breaking her fall and pulling her up and into his arms.

She stared into his dark eyes, reading what would happen all too clearly but not, at this fateful moment, caring. Her eyes drifted closed as he covered her lips with his in a kiss that shook her to her very soul. Involuntarily she responded, wrapping her arms around him to hold him to her for she wished the kiss to last throughout eternity.

Hitherto unknown but delightful sensations tingled deep within her, causing her to press herself closer to him. She wanted more and more and more.

"Ashley," he whispered against her lips. "Your name is as lovely as you are."

But Ashley was *not* her name. That fact cut through her fogged mind like the sun through haze. He was not kissing her, he was kissing Ashley.

Alcida struggled to free herself and almost immediately he released her. Weak-kneed, she leaned against the tunnel wall while she straightened her riding hat and made a less successful attempt to order her emotions.

"That should not have occurred, sir." Despite her best effort, her voice quivered.

"On the contrary. We both enjoyed it."

Since she had responded so wantonly, she could not deny the truth in his allegation. "Nevertheless, such a thing must not happen again." Alcida was pleased to hear the firmness in her tone. "I am here to teach your daughter, not to—to—" She hesitated, unable to find words she was not embarrassed to say to him.

"To become my mistress?"

Put so bluntly, the idea revolted her. "I will not!" She cried.

He smiled slightly. "We shall see."

She frowned at him. How could she have been so sap-witted as to permit him to kiss her? "No, we shan't see, sir." Brushing past him, she marched back the way they had come.

Lady Clematis did most of the talking on the ride back to the house.

Though Alcida remained on the alert for the remainder of the day and evening, the duke made no effort to take up where they had left off. She set her traps in her bedchamber again that night, but no one disturbed them.

She woke early despite a restless night, her sleep plagued by dreams of being in his arms. I shall throw myself into the role of governess, she vowed, and stay completely away from him.

Accordingly, after Janet helped her dress, she sought out the library, finding the paneled room with its wall to ceiling glassed-in bookshelves as dark as all the rest of the rooms in the house. Recklessly flinging open the heavy draperies, she caught them back with their gold cords. Muted light shining through the shrubbery brightened the room to some extent. She was pleased to discover the books had been cataloged fairly recently and soon was able to locate the flora and fauna shelves. To her disappointment, however, there was no book on wildflowers.

She was about to leave when it occurred to her to look for the book about the secret passages that Lady Clematis had spoken of. After a false start—it was not on the shelf dealing with Humber's Harp—she found it in the general architecture section. The information and diagrams soon fascinated her, and she became engrossed in reading about the various secret ways to creep about the huge place.

Many of the passageways connected. One opened directly behind the harp in the entry hall and another led to the tower. Lady Clematis had offered to take her on a tour of the house today but had added that they could not visit the tower. "The tower is Papa's," the girl had confided. "I don't go there except by his invitation."

"You seem to have found something of interest." The duke's voice startled her into almost dropping the book, for she had not heard him enter the room.

"Just browsing," she told him, quickly returning the slim volume to its proper place and hoping he would not discover what she had been reading. Like as not, he would consider the book a private family document, not to be idly perused by an employee.

"I noticed your library does not contain a wildflower book," she informed him.

He frowned. "We must remedy that. I shall be traveling to London on the morrow, and I will bring several back with me."

"Thank you, sir. I am sure your daughter will appreciate them, as will I." She watched him warily as she spoke because he was between her and the door, which he had shut, trapping her alone with him in the library.

"I have told Hancock I shall be leaving my daughter in your care until my return, which should be no more than a few days," he said. "She seems to have formed an attachment to you, which pleases me." He smiled. "I quite understand her feeling."

His last few words led her to believe he might be leading up to another embrace, and she sought for something to distract him, determined not to allow him near her because if he got too close she might not be able to trust herself.

"The harp," she said, seizing on the first thing that came into her mind. "Do you play the harp?"

He shook his head. "No living person has played the harp in years."

No living person—a most peculiar choice of words. Was he implying that ghostly hands sometimes plucked the harp's strings? She was not brave enough to ask. Trying not to be obvious, she began to edge her way slowly around him, eager to escape. " 'Tis a beautiful instrument," she said.

"You are from the neighborhood, so I assume you have heard the tittle-tattle about the First Duke of Roxton, how he still returns to play his harp. Am I correct?"

She nodded, having heard the story from her sister.

"You may on occasion hear the sound of a harp string. I freely admit to you that I have no idea what or who causes the sound." He shrugged. "Perhaps old John Humber does walk the halls at night."

"Because he sold his soul to the devil?" The question was out before she could stop herself.

He raised an eyebrow. "Is that the current story? Most inventive. One cannot countenance it, of course. Had there been a way to call up the devil and sell my soul to him, I would have done just that some years ago."

She stared at him, nonplused. "Whatever for?"

All expression left his face. "Ask the tittle-tattlers. Apparently they know more than I do about my family affairs." Swinging about on his heel, he strode from the room.

She had certainly touched on a sore spot where he was concerned, while succeeding in upsetting herself as well. What tangled coil would lead a man even to think about selling his soul to the devil?

The duke did not appear for the evening meal, nor did Alcida see him before he left in the morning. Instead of feeling relieved that he had gone to London, she found she missed him.

On the third day of his absence, she said to Lady Clematis, "Since your father will be bringing us wildflower books, we might begin to prepare ourselves for studying them by taking our sketchbooks and going for an afternoon ride, stopping to draw any interesting blooms we come across."

"A marvelous idea. And I know the very best place to go. That is, if we can rid ourselves of the groom. I refuse to take him to my favorite spot."

"Your father would not be pleased to hear we slipped away to go riding without an escort."

Lady Clematis made a face. "I rather think I can trust you not to tattle on me, but I cannot trust the groom. Even if I bribe him, he will tell Papa. I suppose he will have to trail after us."

"I see no alternative. Since your father left you in my custody, I cannot in good faith countenance a departure from his rules. We shall just have to do our best to pretend the groom is not with us."

The sun was still high when Alcida and Lady Clematis reached the stables, carrying a small basket the cook had packed for them as well as a sketching parcel. "Please saddle my mare," the girl ordered. "And bring out Ceres for Miss Douglas."

The stablehand hesitated. "Ceres, Lady Clematis?"

"Did you not hear me?" She asked haughtily.

He nodded, mumbled an apology, and set out to do as she bid.

"Ceres?" Alcida echoed sotto voce when he was out of hearing.

"The poor thing hardly ever gets any exercise," the girl said. "You will be doing her a favor. She is not at all difficult to handle."

Alcida subsided, deciding not to create a fuss about what horse she rode, even though she was almost certain that, for some reason she was unaware of, Lady Clematis should not have ordered Ceres saddled for her.

Ceres turned out to be a strikingly colored mare, dappled gray, with an almost white mane and tail. As promised, she proved easy to handle, though inclined to prance a bit, no doubt because she had not been ridden enough lately. With a young groom plodding along behind them, they set off from the stables.

"Where we going, Lady Clematis?" he called.

" 'Tis a surprise for Miss Douglas, so I cannot tell you," she replied.

Because Ceres was pulling at the bit, wanting to run, Alcida suggested they increase their pace a bit so the mare could work off some of her eagerness. To Alcida's dismay, Lady Clematis's answer was to urge Electra into a full gallop. She had no choice but to follow suit, intending to catch up to the girl and urge her to slow her mare. While Lady Clematis was a skilled horsewoman, galloping could prove dangerous.

Ceres all but flew over the field, pulling even with the girl's mare in record time. Alcida was about to call to the girl when a hoarse shout from behind them caused her to glance around. To her horror, both the groom and his mount were on the ground. She reined in Ceres, talking quietly to the mare as she slowed her, then wheeled about to make her way back to the groom.

Lady Clematis evidently had seen the accident, because she passed Alcida, still galloping Electra, and reached the fallen groom first. The groom was sitting up and she was kneeling beside him when Alcida dismounted. Beside them the horse began struggling to its feet.

"Are you hurt, Yonnie?" the girl asked.

"Don't seem so, Milady. More stunned like." He looked around. "Be the horse all right?"

Lady Clematis rose, hurried over to the groom's horse and began speaking softly to him as she ran her hands over his body. The groom pushed himself onto his feet and walked slowly over to join her. He took the reins from the girl and led the animal ahead.

As he did so, it became obvious the horse was favoring his right foreleg.

"Stepped in a rabbit hole, he did," the groom said. "Nothing for it but to walk him back and poultice that leg."

" 'Twas fortunate we had not ridden very far," Alcida observed.

"Take him to the stable, then, Yonnie," Lady Clematis ordered. "Miss Douglas and I will ride around a bit before we return."

Yonnie, apparently too concerned about the horse to worry about the two ladies riding unaccompanied—or perhaps he was still a bit dazed—nodded his agreement. After helping them to remount, he turned the limping horse toward home.

Lady Clematis set off at a sedate pace. "I would never wish any person or animal ill," she said, "and I am relieved that the accident was no worse—neither man nor horse shed a single drop of blood. Still, what happened did free us of Yonnie's presence, did it not?"

Alcida pondered what to do. Should she insist they return to the house?

"I pray you will not tell me that we cannot go on with our ride," the girl said. "I am sure Papa will understand that we did not defy him."

Alcida was not so sure. The sun shone warmly on her shoulders, birds warbled in the trees, some swooping after flying insects, the summery smell of grass mixed with the sweet perfume of clover—all this tempted her to go on and enjoy the beautiful afternoon. Yet she had been left in charge of Lady Clematis.

She bit her lip, torn between want-to and ought-to. Ought-to was winning when without warning Lady Clematis again kicked Electra into a gallop, heading directly away from the house. The choice temporarily taken from her, Alcida pounded after her.

Ceres, clearly a faster horse than the girl's mare, soon pulled even and would have passed the other animal had not Alcida slowed her. "Do stop," she called to Lady Clematis. "Or at least slow your mare. This fast pace is dangerous."

"I will slow down if you agree we can go on," the girl called back to her.

"I am persuaded we should not."

The girl turned a set face toward her. "Then I will keep Electra galloping."

Having witnessed one horse and rider accident already, Alcida feared what might happen to the girl. "Very well," she said reluctantly. "I will at least agree to discuss the matter."

Lady Clematis immediately reined in her mare. When both horses had settled into a more sedate trot, she said, "We are almost there." She pointed to a clump of trees. "That is Gypsy Grove, where the pool is hidden."

Her sister's confession about wading in some other secret pool with Lord Damon flashed through Alcida's mind. Though it had been a rash thing for Ashley to do, considering his reputation, she had understood she might have done the same if tempted by the right man. Was he Thomas Farrington, Eighth Duke of Roxton?

"You are smiling," the girl commented. "Does that mean you agree to go on to the pool?"

After all, they were so close. What was the harm in pausing briefly to view Lady Clematis's hidden pool before riding back? She nodded.

They entered the grove, threaded between the willow and oak trees, and came upon a tiny glade with a small pond in its midst, a blue gem in a setting of greenery.

"How lovely," Alcida said.

"I knew you would like it." Lady Clematis pulled her mare alongside a large rock and slid off her back. Looking up at Alcida, she said, "I am sorry I ran off the way I did. I know it was wrong. But you began biting your lip, and when you do that, I have learned, you are trying to decide what to do. If you had ordered me to return, I should have had to go back, and I so wanted to show the pool to you. 'Tis my very favorite place."

Alcida dismounted, realizing she should scold the girl, even though she had been completely disarmed by her confession. "I am relieved that you understand you should not have set Electra into a gallop," she said mildly. "I do find this a nonpareil spot, but we can stay only a minute or two."

"Long enough to wade? I am perishingly hot."

"Well . . ." Alcida paused, noting that the girl, her riding boots already off, was hitching up her skirts and preparing to peel down her stockings. "I suppose a few more minutes won't matter," she admitted.

"Join me?"

Alcida, heated from the ride under the warm June sun, could think of no reason not to.

* * *

"You left them where?" Roxton's voice throbbed with anger.

Yonnie eyed him furtively before turning back to the horse he was treating. "Said I was sorry, sir," he mumbled. "Guess me wits got addled from the tumble."

Aware he was taking out his ire at Ashley Douglas on the groom, Roxton made an effort to calm himself. "Glad you were not hurt any worse," he said gruffly. "You say they were headed east but refused to tell you where?"

"Gypsy Grove, sir, that's what I think."

Roxton nodded. Quite likely. The place fascinated his daughter. What was Ashley thinking of to go off with Clematis unaccompanied by a groom when she knew it would be against his wishes? Damn and blast the woman. She could not be trusted any more than— He sliced that thought off abruptly.

He started for Zeus, being saddled for him by a stablehand, then paused, staring in disbelief at Ceres's empty stall. "Which horse was Miss Douglas riding?" he demanded.

"Lady Clematis ordered Ceres saddled, sir," the man said, not looking at him. He stood back, mutely offering the mount to Roxton.

Roxton clamped his jaw shut so as not to heap blame on a servant who was merely obeying an order. Clematis knew better. Was she deliberately antagonizing him? she had always been a tractable child, so he could only assume the arrival of Miss Douglas was responsible for her changed behavior. Fuming, he swung onto Zeus.

He had been attracted to Ashley from the first time

he'd noticed her at the market in Louth. She had been a vision of lovely innocence, totally unaware of her beauty. Now that he had brought her within his reach, his desire to possess her had increased until he ached for her. Never mind how he hungered for her, she had failed him and he refused to tolerate a woman he could not trust. He would see she left Humber's Harp this very day.

He fed his anger all the way to the grove. As he entered the trees, the feminine laughter he heard made the fire burn hotter. He slid off Zeus and stomped through the grove in a flaming rage. When he reached the glade he was beyond reason.

Taking no heed of the beauty around him, he marched to the edge of the pond. Some few yards from him, wading up to their thighs in the water, their backs to him, Ashley sported with Clematis as though she, too, were still a child.

Even more inflamed by the enticing glimpse of her white thighs, he roared, "What do you think you are doing?"

Both swerved about to face him. Clematis kept her footing but Ashley stepped backward, lost her balance, and went under. A fitting punishment, he told himself, waiting for her to resurface.

Clematis screamed, causing him to take an involuntary step into the water. "Papa," she cried, "Miss Douglas will drown!"

"Nonsense, the water is shallow."

"No, no, she stepped off the ledge."

At that moment Ashley's face and shoulders broke the surface. For an instant she splashed, sputtering and coughing, and then she sank once more.

"Help, Papa, she cannot swim."

Neither could Clematis. "Get into shore," he ordered as he yanked off his boots. "Now!"

Without bothering to remove anything more than his jacket, he plunged into the water.

Eleven

In the field near Hyde Park, Ashley stared into Lord Damon's dark eyes, unable to determine whether her light-headedness was due to being in his arms or from her near brush with disaster. " 'Twas the chicken's fault," she told him.

He appeared puzzled. Bringing his mount to a halt, he eased her onto the saddle as he dismounted, then pulled her down, catching her in his arms once again. "Are you able to stand by yourself?" he asked.

She felt so warm and safe in his embrace that she did not wish to move. "Um," she murmured.

"Was that a yes or a no?"

Regretfully, she eased away, saying, "I believe I am quite all right." But she was not, for she swayed even as she spoke.

Lord Damon put an arm around her waist. "Lean against me," he advised.

She obeyed, savoring his familiar scent, so well remembered from earlier encounters.

"What did you say about a chicken?" he asked.

"Actually, 'twas the feathers that spooked Mal."

"Mal being your mount?"

"He is as tractable as can be otherwise. I do hope he has not come to harm."

"He is safe. I can see him from here, placidly grazing. I take it you encountered a chicken in the road."

"The pig did not bother him in the slightest, but the chicken—" She paused and sighed. "Before I knew what happened, Mal had bolted. How providential that you were close enough to notice I was in desperate need of help."

"I admit to following you." His arm tightened around her waist.

The sound of horse's hooves alerted her to someone's approach. She pulled free of Lord Damon and turned to see Freddie pounding up on his pony. Good heavens, she had forgotten he was with her.

"Be ye all right, Miss?" he asked. "This 'ere nag's a prize slowcoach, thought I'd never get 'ere."

"Miss Blayne is recovering," Lord Damon answered. "You might bring her horse to her, there's a good lad."

"Seen what ye did, sir," Freddie said admiringly. "Slick's a willow whistle, 'ow ye grabbed 'er off that old 'orse. Saved 'er, ye did."

"Oh, Freddie, I was so fortunate Lord Damon saw Mal bolt," Ashley said. "He is indeed brave." She smiled at her rescuer.

What a charming smile she has, Damon thought, made even more enticing by that dimple in her left cheek. He blinked, aware his thought had triggered a memory. What was it? Something about a smile. . . .

"Ye think she oughta ride Mal back to the 'ouse, sir?" Freddie asked, distracting him.

"With the two of us keeping an eye out for chickens and other feathered creatures she should do fine," Damon said.

"I'll go get 'im, then."

Damon shook his head as he watched Freddie ride off. "He appears devoted to you, but the boy does seem an odd choice for a footman."

"Country lads take a while to adjust to London ways," she said. "Freddie is loyal, and loyalty is one virtue that cannot be bought." She put a hand to her head, causing Damon to step forward, alarmed.

"Vertigo?" he asked with concern, hoping she wasn't about to swoon. She had done remarkably well so far. Whatever else she might be, Alcida Blayne was neither faint-hearted nor prone to the vapors.

"No, no, I was merely attempting to discover if I still have my hat. I had not thought about it until now."

"I assure you the hat is in place. A shame, really, to cover those lively copper curls."

"Copper, sir?

"Come to think on it, copper would better describe young Freddie's hair. Yours is a somewhat darker red, a glorious color, whatever it is." He briefly fingered a curl by her cheek, savoring its softness and the way it tried to cling to his fingers. If only she were as responsive to his touch.

He had thoroughly enjoyed holding her in his arms until she recovered her equilibrium and had found it difficult to let her go. He intended to hold her again as soon as possible—but for a very different reason.

Watching Freddie ride up with Mal on lead, he said to her, "Are you quite certain you feel up to mounting your misbehaving horse again?"

"Mal is not so bad as his name suggests," she replied. "Just keep our feathered friends away from him, please."

They reached her small house without incident. Once there, Damon helped her off the horse and handed the reins to Freddie before escorting her to the door.

"If you will permit me to call on you tomorrow afternoon," he said, "and drive with me to the park, perhaps we shall encounter Lady Jersey and finally be properly introduced."

She raised her eyebrows. "Ride with you before the introduction? Although I suppose my rescue was an introduction of sorts."

"I would venture to say it counts as such."

"I am terribly grateful, you know. I shudder to think of what might have occurred had you not intervened."

"Grateful enough to ride with me on the morrow?"

She smiled shyly. "You have convinced me I must."

He took her hand, bringing it to his lips, looking into her eyes all the while. How green they were, warm and tender, eyes that welcomed him, lured him. He hated to leave her, now understanding what was meant by feeling as though you had to tear yourself away.

"Until then," he said.

When he remounted, he found he did not wish to return to the park and the crush there, he wanted to be alone.

"Sir?" Freddie's voice.

He looked down to see the boy standing by his horse's head. "Yes?"

"Miss Ash—Miss Alcida, she's a real lady, she is, sir. Give me life for 'er I would."

Was this young whelp warning him off? He glared at the boy.

Freddie gulped visibly. "Sorry, sir, but I 'ad to say it. Didn't mean no offense."

The humor of the situation struck Damon. The lad reminded him of a weanling pup trying to protect its mistress from harm. "Quite all right," he said. "Loyalty is all too rare in this world."

As he rode away, he told himself that Alcida was an unusual woman. 'Twas no wonder the boy adored her; she was indeed a nonpareil. He fully intended to treat her as a lady, even after he had won her over and set her up in an establishment worthy of her talent and beauty. God, how he ached for her.

Ashley woke to gray skies and a morning drizzle, but the dismal weather could not dampen her spirits. Wrong or right, she would ride with Lord Damon today. What was the harm in it, after all? She wanted to so very much. How handsome he was, and how brave—top-o'-the-trees, just as Freddie had once said.

If she had relived the rescue once, she had relived it a hundred times, especially the part about being in his arms. How strong and fearless he was.

Later that morning, as she sat in the parlor with her embroidery, Ursula entered and said, "I hope you realize you have held that needle in the same position for the last half hour."

Ashley started, coming out of a reverie where she and Lord Damon were waltzing at a ball—her first waltz, as he had requested. "You shall never waltz with any man but me," he had just told her.

"A flirtation is one thing," Ursula cautioned, "an infatuation quite another. Alcida knew the difference, but I am not persuaded that you do."

"I am not infatuated with Lord Damon," Ashley declared indignantly.

"No? What would you call it?"

"Why I—I like him, of course."

"Of course." Ursula smiled wryly. "Next you will tell me you do not long for his kiss."

Ashley flushed, putting a hand to her reddening cheek. "Is that so terrible?" She asked, knowing she'd given herself away. She stabbed the needle into the cloth. "What harm is there in a kiss?"

"In the actual kiss, none. In what the kiss leads to, much more misery than you can imagine."

Ashley stared at her. "You cannot believe I would permit him—or any man—undue liberties!"

"Any man, no. Lord Damon, quite possibly, given time. He is well-set-up, charming, and determined to have you. Or, rather, Alcida."

Her sister's name struck Ashley like a blow. She had managed rather conveniently to forget who Lord Damon believed she was. He had never once kissed Ashley Douglas. Even back in Lincolnshire when he'd kissed her he had thought she was her sister.

Just the same, she consoled herself, I was always the one he kissed, whether he knew it or not. But she was not comforted. When she and Alcida had planned the masquerade with Lady Lancaster, everything had seemed so simple. How could she have known what a devilish coil would result?

"I shall take your advice to heart," she assured Ursula, meaning every word. " 'Twould be the height of folly to allow my head to be turned by a—a rake. I shall take care to treat him in the manner that my sister might."

After observing her for a moment or two, Ursula nodded. "I am persuaded you mean to try, difficult as it may prove to be for you. I have one suggestion that may help remind you of what you mean to do and that is to always assume any gentleman of the *ton* who courts you is merely attempting to bed you. This being true, you cannot trust one word they utter, for in order to accomplish their desire, they scatter sweet-sounding falsehoods at your feet like rose petals."

Ashley stared at the older woman. Despite her graying hair and her certain age, Ursula was still a handsome woman. Was she speaking from experience? Had she not mentioned loving and losing?

Ursula smiled thinly. "I can see you are wondering how an old, on-the-shelf spinster like me can possibly know these things." She raised a hand as Ashley started to sputter a denial. "Strange as it may seem to you, I was once young, innocent, and reasonably attractive. My friends in the theater troupe did their utmost to protect me, but nothing they said or did could prevent me from running off with the gentleman I lost my heart to.

"I believed him when he told me he intended to marry me; indeed, I understood we *were* married because one of his friends pretended to be a clergyman and conducted a mock service."

Ashley was horrified. "How cruel!"

Ursula sighed. "My happiness was short-lived, for

the announcement of his engagement to an earl's daughter was published less than a year later. When I confronted him, he admitted we had never been truly wed. He then told me he had every intention of continuing to support me and saw no reason we could not go on as we were, since, he said, he did not expect to enjoy his wife in the same way he enjoyed me. He could not understand my refusal and he never did realize he had broken my heart."

Overcome by sympathy, Ashley set her sewing aside, rose, crossed to Ursula and embraced her. The older woman hugged her back, then said, "While I still cherish the brief happiness I experienced, I would not wish to suffer such misery again as I did from that escapade. That is why I cannot stand idly by and watch you make a similar mistake. Remember, when Lord Damon marries, it will be to a woman who comes from the aristocracy, a woman who can trace her faultless and noble bloodlines back for many generations."

Ashley had known this from the moment she'd met him on the bank of Dane's Run but had chosen to banish it from her thoughts. Now she was forced to think about it. The room brightened as the sun struck through the clouds and cast a shaft of light through the parted curtains of the parlor. But no light could brighten the darkness clouding Ashley's heart.

"I cannot possibly go riding with him this afternoon," she said.

"On the contrary, you must. Avoiding him will solve nothing, for he will continue the chase. Sooner or later you will have to learn how to deal with these false-hearted gentlemen of the *ton,* and you may as well practice with Lord Damon. Once you have conquered your *tendresse* for him, you will never be affected so acutely again."

Ashley was sure Ursula was right, but oh, she did not want to be with Lord Damon, knowing every word he spoke to her was a lie.

" 'Tis a game to them," Ursula said. "Make it a game two can play."

A game. Taking a deep breath, Ashley let it out slowly. She must try, but 'twas a game she wished with all her heart she did not have to learn to play.

For the first time since they had begun the masquerade, she wondered if Alcida was not the more fortunate of the two of them. Whatever problems her sister might be having at Humber's Harp, falling in love with the sinister duke was surely not one of them.

By the time Lord Damon arrived, Ashley had changed her gown three times, finally settling on the one with the most daring décolletage. Staring at the vision in the entry pier glass, she could almost believe she was not just wearing her sister's clothes but that she *was* Alcida. She certainly did not look like the rustic maiden who had arrived in London less than a fortnight ago.

The gown, a concoction of deep pink sarcenet over a pale pink satin petticoat, gave the clever illusion of revealing skin rather than silk. Rosettes of satin in the same color as the overdress decorated the low neckline and swirled around the edge of the skirt. Her small-brimmed pink bonnet was trimmed with the same rosettes. Pink gloves and a ruffled-edge pink parasol completed the outfit.

Since she had never before owned a parasol, Ashley practiced a few flirtatious twirls in front of the mirror. Naturally she had worn gloves at times in Lincolnshire, but not necessarily every day, and she found them rather a nuisance as they always seemed to pick up every smudge of dirt, even inside this house where Ursula saw to it was kept as spotless as possible.

I will behave exactly like my sister, she told herself firmly, since I *am* Alcida in everyone's eyes. Catching herself gripping the heart locket she always wore around her neck, she shook her head and released it. No matter what the name on the inside of the locket read, Ashley was not the sister who would ride with Lord Damon today.

As Damon halted his blacks in front of Alcida's small house, another rig pulled up behind him. He got down and glared at the man who jumped out of the curricle. "What the deuce are you doing here, Liam?" he growled.

"Meant to try my luck with the beauteous Miss Blayne. See you're ahead of me, as usual. Driving that rig you won from Tiny Tim, ain't you?"

Damon gave a curt nod, refusing to be distracted by the comment about his curricle. "You have not even been introduced to Miss Blayne," he said.

"No more than have you, seeing as how Lady Jersey is out of the city this fortnight. Thought I'd take my chances."

"Did you not win rather heavily at White's last evening?"

"So I did," Liam admitted.

"As my dear departed maternal grandfather was wont to warn, 'Lucky at cards, unlucky in love.' "

"On the other hand, old man, I may be having a run of luck, who can tell? Mean to put it to the test."

Seeing that his friend was not to be easily dislodged, Damon said, "Very well, we shall let the lady choose. But I must warn you that I am expected."

Side by side they marched to the front door, where Damon graciously allowed Liam the honor of raising and lowering the knocker to announce their arrival.

The gray-haired woman called Ursula opened the door. Damon was not quite certain what her status in the household was—perhaps companion might be the appropriate niche.

"Good afternoon, gentlemen," she said, proffering a salver for their cards. "Please follow me."

They found themselves in a parlor so small it seemed crowded with the three of them present. "I shall inform Miss Blayne you are here," Ursula announced.

"She gave no indication you were expected," Liam said, after Ursula had exited.

Damon's only answer was a frown. Not in the least discomfited, Liam extracted an enameled snuffbox from his jacket and opened the top, offering it to Damon, who shook his head. Liam indulged, tucked the box away, and gave a mighty sneeze just as Alcida appeared in the doorway.

"Why, Mr. Gonoud," she exclaimed, smiling at Liam, "what a pleasant surprise. I am delighted to see you." She nodded at Damon. "And you, too, of course, sir."

"I believe you consented to ride with me this afternoon," Damon told her, thinking he'd never seen such a delicious sight as Alcida in the pink confection she wore. She was lovely as a rose, one he longed to pluck.

She slanted him a teasing glance. "Why, I might have done so. But here is Mr. Gounod. What are we to do with him, pray, sir?"

"Send him to the devil" was on his tongue, but he held the words back. Before he found others, she said, "Perhaps Mr. Gounod could ride with us. Would not that be a pleasant solution?"

"Capital!" Liam exclaimed. "I'll just nip out and secure the cattle."

"Be assured my footman will take care of your horses, Mr. Gounod." She beamed impartially at both men.

Trapped, with no polite way out, Damon forced a smile. "Of course I am delighted to offer my good friend the chance to ride with us." He more or less spat the words out from between his teeth.

"The truth is, gentlemen," Alcida said, looking at first one, then the other through her lashes, "that, since I have not been introduced to either of you, I feel my reputation is more secure with two than one. As you know, a lady's reputation can so easily be fatally marred. I fear mine may be smudged already by my accident yesterday. I was in such confusion afterward, I hardly recall getting home, though I believe Lord Damon was responsible for helping me here. Which may have been improper."

The little imp! She knew perfectly well what had happened; this was all a pretense. Was she flirting with Liam to tease him? He suspected so.

"Horse ran away with you, did he?" Liam asked. "Heard Damon played the hero."

"Had you been there, Mr. Gounod, I am convinced you would have done the same. But I pray you shall choose another subject for discussion on our ride. I do not care to be reminded of my accident."

" 'Course you don't. Remarkable you're able to be up and about today."

She favored him with a tremulous smile. "One must go on."

Damon watched Liam swallow her act like a fish taking a lure. Did not the gudgeon remember the girl was not only a singer, but a skilled actress?

"Shall we be off, then?" he asked, a trifle brusquely.

As they walked to the door, Liam hovered over her so solicitously that he, rather than Damon, was the one who placed a colorful Chinese shawl over her shoulders, saying, "Wouldn't do to take a chill, you know."

"You are so thoughtful," she murmured, giving Liam a languishing glance.

Glaring at the two of them, Damon was tempted to bow out and allow then to continue their charade without him as audience. But he was damned if he intended to allow Liam free rein. He would positively enjoy banishing his friend to the tiger's seat on the ride, but unfortunately, the curricle he was driving today had been built wider than most due to the fact that it had originally belonged to Lord Timon, infor-

mally known as Tiny Tim because of his excessiv
avoirdupois. There would be room for three instea
of the customary two, so he could hardly insist Lian
sit in the rear of the rig.

Rather than joust with Liam for the privilege o
assisting Alcida into the curricle, Damon politel
stepped aside and allowed his friend to do the hon
ors. He was well aware that he would, as driver, be in
the middle and so as a matter of necessity would sepa
rate Liam from her.

"Remember when you bought that matched pai
of cattle right out from under my nose at Tatter
sall's?" Liam commented to Damon, once they al
were seated. "Made up my mind then and there to
stop hanging back. Man can't afford to if you're any
where about."

"They *are* handsome horses," Miss Blayne com
mented.

"Damon rarely makes a mistake in what he does,"
Liam said. "Only time I recall seeing him at a los
was last month in the country. Maybe, Miss Blayne
you've heard about how we met a country lass whe
looked as much like you as two peas in a pod do."

"I think I remember some tittle-tattle," she sai
vaguely. Turning toward Damon, she asked, "Wa
that where the young lady pushed you into the rive
because you had annoyed her?"

Liam whooped with laughter.

"I was not pushed," he said, tamping down his an
noyance.

"He claims he tipped the boat over and fell in,"
Liam said, still chuckling. "Not a good day fo
Damon, all 'round."

Neither was today, Damon thought with some irritation, urging his blacks into the flow of traffic on Piccadilly.

"Still, as I recall, he managed to kiss her," Liam added. "So there was some compensation."

"I would wager 'twas against the young lady's wishes," Miss Blayne said.

"You see, he thought she was you," Liam explained.

"Well!" She turned a frosty look on Damon. "How *dare* you?"

Damon blinked, endeavoring to understand why he had been put in the wrong in retrospect. "I can hardly apologize to you," he told Miss Blayne, "because, after all, you were not the Lincolnshire girl I kissed."

"But you thought I was. And you did not even know me." She was obviously miffed.

Wishing Liam at the bottom of an oubliette for bringing up the matter, Damon made another effort to work his way out of the damned coil he had somehow landed in. "I had seen you on-stage," he began, "and heard you sing. As all the men in audience were, I was dazzled by the beautiful Miss Blayne and longed to meet you. Then, suddenly, in the wilds of Lincolnshire, I believed I had come upon you rusticating and I fear I quite lost my head."

"So you took advantage of the poor girl you mistook for me."

"I admit I am ashamed of my behavior." He did his best to look contrite. "Please say you forgive me."

"How can I forgive you when I was not the one you kissed in Lincolnshire?"

Why must she keep dwelling on the incident? In a blue funk, he entered the park. Almost immediately someone in a landau waved at them. Damon recognized her as one of the three Miss Kenilworths—the attractive one.

He stopped the curricle. "Liam," he said, "I do believe Georgianna Kenilworth is trying to attract your attention. 'Twould be impolite to ignore her."

Liam glanced at the landau. "Waltzed with her at the last ball," he said. "Meant to call. Didn't. Haven't seen her since. Nothing for it but to do the pretty." Excusing himself to Miss Blayne, he jumped down and made his way over to the landau.

Damon immediately urged his blacks on.

"Wait," Miss Blayne cried. "You are deserting poor Mr. Gounod."

Damon grinned at her. "And not a moment too soon. Three is definitely a crowd."

"But he has no way to return to collect his curricle at my place!"

"Rest assured that Miss Kenilworth will be more than happy to offer him a ride. He is resisting offering for her, but in the end he will. She is exactly the wife he needs, and he knows she is."

Miss Blayne bit her lip and the gesture seemed oddly familiar to him. Perhaps he had watched her do it before. What was she thinking? Surely she could not be disturbed because he had mentioned that Liam was ripe for marriage. Was she afraid to be alone with him?

"The crush in the park grows worse each year," he said, ignoring several attempts from other carriages to attract his attention. "This has become a horrible squeeze. We shall have to find less-traveled roads."

Without waiting for her agreement or disapproval, he turned off, intending to exit the park. He knew a lovely spot by the Thames where no one would bother them.

"I should like to be taken home," she told him. "I feel quite fatigued. Perhaps the accident did affect me more than I realized at the time."

He could scarcely dismiss such a plea, even though he did not completely believe her. "Of course," he said, plotting in his mind the most roundabout way to get there. " 'I neglected to tell you how charming you look. If I were a musician, I might call you a rhapsody in pink."

She smiled, showing that enticing dimple.

Encouraged, he said, "Though I admit I may have acted impulsively, I shall never regret kissing you."

Turning a startled face to him, she said, "In Lincolnshire?"

"Cannot we forget that mistake in the country?"

"Mistake?"

" 'Twas an honest one. But that was another place and another girl. What I meant was, here in London."

Her expression was so woebegone that he put an arm around her shoulders, drawing her closer. "Have I said something that troubled you?"

For one exquisite moment she leaned against him and he felt her delectable softness. He cursed the busy street and the daylight, wishing for privacy and darkness so that he could pull her into his arms and make love to her.

Pulling away, she sat primly upright. "Are you, like Mr. Gounod, about to announce your engagement?" she asked.

Surprised, he shook his head.

"Because you haven't found your Miss Kenilworth, or because you do not intend to marry?" she went on.

Whatever had persuaded her into a discussion of his readiness to wed or not to wed? She should not be asking such questions.

"I have no plans to marry in the near future," he said stiffly.

"And when you do, it will not be to me." Her words shocked him speechless.

She further upset him by bursting into tears. What in hell was he supposed to do now? If her drove her home in this condition, it would be all over town that he had abused Miss Blayne, causing her to weep all over his curricle. Making up his mind quickly, he turned into a street that would lead him to a mews in back of Timon's town house. Tiny Tim had left for the Continent yesterday so he would not be there to pass on gossip. And the mews was secluded.

Ashley sobbed into her handkerchief, too miserable to pay any attention to where they were going until she felt the curricle come to a halt. She mopped at her eyes, assuming they were home and she would have to see to get down and run into the house. How could she face him after what she had said? Though it was his own fault she had been driven to do so.

With tear-blurred vision, she stared at unfamiliar surroundings. Stables? Before she had time to think, Lord Damon had pulled her into his arms. She had no heart to struggle free, for she desperately needed comfort. Taking a deep, shuddering breath, she rested her head against his chest.

"You must know I care for you," he murmured, "and would not willingly hurt you." Tipping up her face, he kissed her, gently at first, and then, when she couldn't help but respond, with passionate intensity. Unable to resist her own need, she melted against him, abandoning herself to his caresses.

Twelve

In the grove, while Clematis stood whimpering on the shore, Roxton stumbled out of the pond carrying the limp body of Ashley Douglas in his arms. He sat on the ground, laid her face down across his lap, and began pummeling her back with the sides of his hands.

"What are you doing, Papa?" Clematis cried. "Please don't hurt her."

Roxton paid no attention, continuing the pummeling until the half-drowned woman gave a convulsive gasp. He nodded with satisfaction as water poured from her nose and mouth. A gypsy groom he had once employed had taught him this technique for reviving the drowned. Little had he thought at the time that he would ever use the method. No matter that they were often thieves and liars, gypsies not only knew horses, but they had a grasp of arcane lore unmatched by others.

Ashley began to cough and move spontaneously. He shifted her until she fit into his arms, holding her as one would a child. "Take a deep breath, there's a good girl," he murmured, staring intently into her pale face.

How white her skin was, contrasting starkly with

her sodden auburn hair. Her eyes fluttered open, giving him a glimpse of green before closing again. Even pale and bedraggled she was beautiful, so lovely that he felt a strange pang in the vicinity of his heart.

Clematis, who had hovered fearfully off to his right, ventured closer and kneeled beside him. "Will she be all right, Papa?" she asked.

"I believe she should be," he said. "Cobb told me once the water comes out, there is nothing to worry about. You remember Cobb, don't you?"

"He taught me how to ride." Clematis said.

"He taught me how to save a drowned person. That is what I was doing to Miss Douglas."

"Look, Papa, her eyes are open."

He glanced down at Ashley again and found her gazing up at him, confusion darkening the clear green of her eyes. She coughed again and he propped her into a more erect position.

"Oh, Miss Douglas," Clematis cried, "I thought you had drowned and I was so frightened. But Papa plunged in and saved you."

Comprehension brightened her eyes. "I went under the water," she said in a raspy voice. She gripped Roxton, holding fast to him as though fearing to be swept under again.

Up until this moment his attention had been fixed on saving her, but now that she was alert and clinging to him, her soft curves against his body, he felt the stirrings of desire, and involuntarily his arms tightened about her.

"Papa, I'm cold."

Brought back to the moment by his daughter's wail, Roxton's need changed to concern for her and for the woman he held. He must get them back to the house as quickly as possible, or in their wet clothes they would take a chill. He was soaked to the skin himself and it was damned uncomfortable despite the warm day.

As he rose, still holding Ashley, the rumble and creaking of wheels came to his ears. Carrying her, with Clematis trailing him, he hurried through the grove, spotted a hay cart crossing a field, and hailed the driver, Josh Whitcombe, one of his tenant farmers.

After Josh drove the cart close, Roxton laid Ashley onto the straw, covered her with his dry jacket, then lifted his daughter in. He tied Electra to the tail of the cart, ordered Clematis to keep an eye on both her governess and her mare, then told Josh to drive to the house.

Returning to the grove, he led Ceres to where Jupiter was waiting, mounted the stallion, and rode off with Ceres on lead. It was the first time in three years he had been anywhere near his wife's mare.

As he pounded toward the house, shivering as the breeze blew past his wet clothes, fragments of the past surfaced despite his efforts to keep them under.

"Don't put the mare down, Master," Cobb had begged as Roxton put his pistol to Ceres' head. " 'Tain't her fault; she be animal, not human."

He could not bring himself to shoot the horse, for if anyone was guilty, he himself was. Ceres still lived, while Madeline, his wife, lay three years under the turf.

Shaking off these bitter memories, he focused his thoughts on what to do once he reached the house:

have Hancock mobilize the staff to take care of Clematis and Ashley, then send for the doctor.

When he got there and made certain everything would be in readiness for their care, Frederick, his valet, had to remind him twice to change his wet clothes before riding back to see where the much slower haycart was.

"Won't do no good should you catch your death, Milord," Frederick chided.

Recognizing the logic but chafing at the delay, Roxton hurried the valet through the process and was preparing to remount Zeus when one of the grooms ran up, shouting that he had spotted the cart.

As it creaked its way into the stableyard he hurried toward it, seeing Clematis and Ashley huddled together amidst the straw, looking wan and bedraggled. "Are you all right?" he demanded.

Teeth chattering, Ashley said, "I think so. I am sorry, sir, for endangering your daughter."

" 'Tis my fault, Papa," Clematis cried. "I teased and teased until Miss Douglas agreed to go wading."

"We won't assign blame at the moment," Roxton said. "You both must have a hot bath and be put into a warm bed with a hot drink."

His father's remedy for any and all illnesses had been whiskey mixed with honey and diluted with boiling water. Roxton ordered this mixture made and took it upstairs himself once he'd been informed his daughter and her governess were in bed.

Clematis made a face when he appeared with the whiskey mix, for she had encountered it before during various illnesses. With her abigail hovering over her, holding the mixture, she made no objection to swallowing it. He bent and kissed her, then carried the second mug in to Ashley's bedchamber.

She was alone in the room, looking tiny and frail in the bed, her auburn curls bright against the white of the pillow. Feeling the same peculiar tug in his chest at the sight of her, he set the mug on the bedside stand and pulled up a chair.

"This is my father's famous cure-all," he said rather brusquely, lifting the mug and offering it to her.

She eased onto one elbow, took the mug, brought it to her lips, took a sip, and gasped. "Heavens, what is this?"

"Drink it down," he ordered. "Clematis took hers without any fuss."

"I am not your daughter, sir." Nevertheless, she took several more sips before setting the mug back onto the stand. "Am I now to be subjected to a well-deserved dressing down?" she asked.

He shook his head, hardly recalling how angry he had been at her audacity. When he had carried her from the water, fearing she was dead, he had understood she was not a passing fancy. Somehow she had gotten under his skin to the extent that he knew he must not lose her. His life, barren before her arrival, would be intolerable without her presence.

He had vowed never to marry again, but that would be no problem because wedding Ashley was not what he had in mind—she would not be an appropriate wife. He wanted her as his mistress and he meant to have her. Something would have to be done about keeping the relationship from Clematis—perhaps sending her away to school for a year or so. She had asked to go once, but at the time he had not taken to the idea of allowing her out of his sight.

"Cannot you find the proper words to dress me down?" Ashley asked.

"Finish your medicine," he ordered, pointing to the mug, secretly delighted that she felt well enough to revert to her pert comments.

She scowled at him as she lifted the mug for a few more sips. "I do not care for the taste. Still, I suppose the nastier the flavor, the more effective the remedy."

When she set the mug down he grasped her hand, holding it between his. "I cannot find it in my heart to chastise you for I, too, have experienced my daughter's wheedling ways. I thank God you are both safe and sound."

"Thanks to you, sir. I do not recall you carrying me from the water, though I am aware you did. All I remember is going under and then waking up to find you looking into my eyes. It was like a pleasant dream replacing a horrible nightmare."

Alcida knew very well she should remove her hand from his. She could not. When he touched her she felt safe and warm. And more, though at the moment she did not care to examine what the more consisted of. She smiled at him, happy he had chosen to sit with her for a time. She enjoyed his company more than she had any other man's.

Looking into those dark, dark eyes, she felt herself falling, falling into a deep, bottomless pool, not of water but of glowing fire that tingled rather than burned. He leaned closer and her lips parted in anticipation. When he kissed her the tingling increased, settling deep inside her and creating an urgent desire to be in his arms, held close against him.

His lips were warm and insistent, taking possession of not only her mouth but all of her. She felt she belonged to him, that he was the only man in the world for her.

A tapping at the door ended the wonderful caress. She sank back against her pillows with a sigh as the duke rose and bade the person enter. Hancock appeared. "Dr. Higgins is with Lady Clematis, Milord. I have taken the liberty of summoning Miss Douglas's maid to be at her bedside when the doctor visits."

"Very good, Hancock. I shall see the doctor in the library when he is finished." Turning to her, he added formally, "I trust you will suffer no ill effects from your dunking, Miss Douglas."

And then he was gone. For Alcida it was as though every candle and lamp in the house had guttered out, leaving her in darkness.

What is happening to me? she asked herself. I cannot possibly be falling in love with the Eighth Duke—that would be preposterous! As well as extremely hen-witted. Why did I agree to this charade, anyway? No doubt my sister is having the time of her life in London, flirting with all the gentlemen and not losing her heart to any of them. Lucky Ashley.

Dr. Higgins was his usual cheerful self. "Fell into a pond, did we?" he asked jovially. "You seem none the worse for it at the moment, but we shall take precautions. You must remain in bed at least for a day, preferably two, to avoid the chance of lung fever."

"Oh, dear," she said. "I am supposed to be teaching Lady Clematis."

"As she reminded me," the doctor said. "I have given her permission to come into your bedchamber for an hour or two each day. She can share your bed, well wrapped against a chill, and you may instruct her as you wish, keeping in mind not to strain the intellectual powers while you both are bedridden."

After the doctor left, Janet fetched Alcida a light meal from the kitchen, which she ate with good appetite. Afterward she fell asleep, exhausted by the day's events, never once thinking about placing her improvised alarms in front of the door and the secret panel.

Sometime in the night, Alcida roused, certain she had heard a noise. As nearly as she could tell with the bedside lamp burning low, she was alone. Her bellpull lay close at hand to summon Janet, but she did not need any help at the moment; she only wished to know what had roused her. She raised her head, listening, and heard the wind moaning past her window as it swept across the wold. Such a wild wind must mean a storm was on the way. Quite possibly its wailing had awakened her.

She was settling herself to try to sleep again when she heard another sound, a musical sound, faint and far away. What was it? When she realized the sound might have come from a stringed instrument, she sat up abruptly. The harp!

At that moment she heard a distinct click, followed by the eerie feeling someone was in her room, though the dim glow of the lamp revealed no one. But shadows obscured the far corners of the room, including the stretch of wainscoting that concealed the secret panel. She could not be sure the panel was closed or that the shadows did not conceal an intruder.

The door, as usual, had come ajar. Was that the click she had heard? Unwilling to sit waiting for what might come, she decided she must take action.

Summon Janet? She shook her head. All Janet could do was look around, and she was perfectly capable of doing that without anyone's help. Assuring herself that she did not believe in ghosts, she gripped the lamp handle and rose from the bed. The leafy vines climbing the brass headboard seemed to squirm in the wavering light, and she shifted her gaze elsewhere. Heart pounding, she advanced toward the secret panel. 'Twas closed. Cautiously she circled the room, lamp in hand, shadows moving with her. She found no one and there was nothing out of place.

Nothing, that is, except the melodious *ping* of a harp string drifting into her room through the partly open door. Before she reached the door, it swung closed with a click. She stood before the door, gathering courage to open it, knowing she must or she would not sleep a wink. Dare she appear in her nightclothes? The gown of Ashley's she was wearing was as high-necked as most of her sister's dresses and of a sturdy cotton not designed to be revealing. She made up her mind to risk it.

When she opened the door, she saw no one, and nothing moved in the gloomy corridor. Holding the lamp up, Alcida took a hesitant step into the corridor, then another and another, until at last she stood at the top of the staircase, staring down into the darkened Great Hall, listening with increasing agitation to the occasional sound of a harp string.

"There are no ghosts," she muttered under her breath. "In any case, ghosts don't play harps."

Something moved in the darkness below. Startled, she emitted a tiny yelp of fright.

"Is that you, Ashley?" the duke's deep voice called up to her.

She released a heartfelt sigh of relief, and not pausing to consider the consequences, padded down the steps. He was waiting at the bottom, still dressed, but without his jacket and with his shirt open at the throat.

"You should not be up wandering around," he scolded.

"I heard the harp."

"Yes. It plays on nights like this."

"Do you mean windy nights?" she asked after a moment. "What actually woke me, I believe now, was the wind blowing my door open, then closed."

"I fear some of our doors do not latch any too well."

The harp pinged again, making her jump. She raised the lamp and looked toward it. "No one is there," she whispered.

"No one is ever there."

Drawn by the enigma of the harp strings being plucked by nobody and taking courage from the duke's presence, she drifted toward the instrument until she stood next to it. If a ghost was near, she certainly did not feel its presence. What she did experience was more mundane. Her bare feet, already cold from the floors, turned numb as she felt the swirl of wind around her legs and feet.

"There is a considerable draft by the harp," she said.

He shrugged. "There is no getting away from the fact this is a drafty old pile."

"The panel," she said without thinking, raising the lamp to examine the wall behind the harp.

The duke was silent for a long moment. "You are," he asked at last, "referring to the secret passageway?"

Since she could not retract her incautious words, there was nothing for it but to plunge on. "Is there not an entrance near the harp?"

"You must have studied the drawings quite closely." His tone suggested that she should not have touched the book, much less opened and perused it.

"Never mind whether I should have looked at them or not," she said impatiently. "Do you not see what conclusion I have reached?"

"You mentioned the secret panel," he said slowly, "and the wind. I admit 'tis within the realm of possibility you are right in your assumption."

"I cannot believe in ghosts," she admitted, "so I was forced to search for another answer. If neither you, Lady Clematis, nor any servant plucked the strings, then what was the cause? My knowledge of the secret panel behind the harp, feeling the draft, and the fact the wind blew my door open and shut gave me the clues. The wind must funnel through the hidden passageway with such force that on nights when the wind is wild, it makes the harp strings quiver enough to be heard."

He laid a hand on her shoulder. "A brilliant deduction, Ashley. 'Tis long past time we laid old John Humber to rest."

How she longed to tell him she was not Ashley, that the gold locket she wore bore her true name inside. But she must not give away the masquerade.

"You are using my given name, sir," she said instead.

"Use mine, then," he countered. "Call me Thomas. At least when we are alone together."

"I cannot, sir."

Ignoring her refusal and apparently noticing her bare feet for the first time, he said, "No slippers? This will never do. You should not be wandering around, especially not barefooted, when the doctor ordered you to rest." So saying, he plucked the lamp from her hand, set it aside, scooped her into his arms, and headed for the staircase.

She clung to him to avoid falling, closing her eyes to relish the feel of being close to him. She breathed in his scent, committing it to memory. How strong he was, and fearless as well. He had saved her life at the risk of his own. She wanted nothing more than to be in his arms forever.

Yet she dared not permit him inside her room. "Sir," she said, hoping he would not notice her breathlessness, "I pray you will put me down outside my door."

"We are not going to your door," he told her. "Or to mine, either, if that is what worries you."

Up another flight of stairs he carried her, up and up in the darkness, winding around and around until they arrived at the top of what she deduced must be the tower. He opened a door and carried her inside a room lit dimly by a hanging oil lamp. Oddly enough, the dimness suited this room, making the furnishings seem mysteriously beautiful.

Depositing her gently upon a chaise longue covered in an Oriental pattern, he sat next to her, taking her cold feet, one at a time, into his hands and chafing them gently. In her entire life, no one had ever caressed her feet before. Along with the pleasure of his touch and the returning warmth, she experienced a languorous longing to have his hands touch her in other, more secret places.

Desperately trying to recover her sense of propriety, she said, "I should not be here, sir."

"Not sir," he said. "We are alone, and my name is Thomas."

A memory flashed into her mind, making her struggle to suppress laughter. Despite her efforts, a giggle escaped. Realizing she would have to explain, she said, "I mean no disrespect, but I fear the name Thomas reminds me of none other than a cat we once rescued." She did not mention that the rescue had been from a London gutter, nor that the cat subsequently became the theater mascot. "I can vividly recall how bedraggled he looked the night we brought him in out of the rain, all wet and miserable."

He smiled. "And named him Thomas, I take it."

She nodded.

He laid her feet back onto the chaise longue, pulled a shawl from its back, and covered her with the shawl from the waist down, tucking it around her.

"You do understand why I cannot call you by your first name?" she asked.

"I was wet enough today to be called bedraggled,"

he told her. "And I have always admired the fierce independence of tomcats. You may not realize it, but you have, in a way, rescued me. So I see no problem."

" 'Tis not really because of the cat, as you must know."

He leaned over her, one arm to either side of her head, his nearness tripling her heartbeat. "I should like to hear my name on your lips," he said softly.

Unable to resist his plea, she whispered, "Thomas."

"Again."

"Thomas." The name had barely slipped out before he covered her lips with his.

Though she wanted above all to drown in his kiss, Alcida marshalled the power of her will and thrust her hands between them, pushing against his chest until he released her enough so she could speak. "I pray you will not do this, for I do not wish to become a ruined woman."

"I will take care of you," he promised.

She shook her head.

"I can sense you enjoy my caresses," he said with a strange huskiness in his voice that sent off skyrockets inside her.

A brilliant greenish-white light suddenly lit the tower room and almost immediately came the crash of thunder. Wind rattled the windows, sending rain splattering against the glass.

The storm was upon them. There was also a storm within her, flashing strange urges throughout her body that could be assuaged only by allowing him to hold her close. She did not dare give in to this longing. Whether she called him sir or His Grace or

Thomas would make no difference. He was still the Eighth Duke of Roxton, while she was a London songbird, singing for her living, an orphan with unknown bloodlines. He would never marry her and she was not willing to become any man's mistress. Even if she loved him.

Thirteen

In his curricle, clasped in Lord Damon's arms, dazed by his caresses, Ashley struggled to recall the promise she had made to Ursula no more than a few short hours ago. One kiss leads to another, Ursula had warned, and, eventually, to ruin. But oh, 'twas difficult to worry about being ruined when his lips were so warm and his touch so delightful.

His mouth left hers to trail around to her ear, and with great effort, she managed to gasp, "Lord Damon, I—"

He cut her off, whispering in her ear, "Charles, please call me Charles." His hot breath tickled her ear, thrilling her and undermining her will. "And I shall call you Alcida," he added.

Hearing her sister's name brought back her sanity. She pulled away from him, one hand going up to clasp her heart locket, holding it tightly as if to remind her of who she really was. "Sir, we must not," she said, wishing her voice was firm rather than breathless. "I have no desire to be ruined."

He gazed at her with an eyebrow raised. "My dear girl, you must know I would take care of you."

Ashley edged over to the far side of the curricle

seat. "I don't intend to become any man's bit o' muslin," she told him. "Not even yours."

He appeared bemused. "Not even mine?" he repeated.

"Well," she blurted, "if I were ever to consider such a scandalous arrangement, I would rather 'twas with you." Only after the words were out did she realize how much she had admitted to him. Her face burned with embarrassment. Why, she had all but told him outright that she loved him!

He shook his head. "I cannot be certain anything you say is genuine. You have just given me the perfect portrayal of an innocent, except for the slip when you mentioned 'bit o' muslin.' No true innocent would know the word, let alone what it meant. What an actress you are, right down to an actual blush."

She wanted to cry that 'twas not an act, but she held her tongue, remembering who she was supposed to be. Her sister, after all, could be considered an actress. As for innocents, he did not know as much about them as he imagined he did.

"If you did not wish to make love in a mews, why not be honest about it?" he asked.

For Ashley, his words spoiled all that had just now happened between them. His kisses had made her forget her surroundings, but they were undeniably in a mews. "I don't wish to make love with you anywhere!" she cried, looking straight ahead so he would not see the tears she was blinking back. "Please take me home immediately."

Damon cursed his ineptness as he turned the horses about in order to leave Tiny Tim's mews. What was there about this woman that made him forget all the clever seduction techniques he had learned? The trouble was he was too eager to possess her. Make love in a mews, indeed! What had he been thinking of? Liam would laugh himself sick if word ever got out, then would share the joke with everyone.

She was definitely on her high horse, chin in the air, staring anywhere but at him. 'Twould be a while before he would be admitted to her good graces again. As he pondered his next move, he saw a flower vendor on the corner ahead of them. Reining in the horses, he flipped the woman a couple of shillings, leaned down, plucked the rose bouquet from her hand, and offered it to Alcida.

"My abject apologies," he murmured. "I have no defense other than the fact that you drive me to distraction."

Holding the white roses, she bent her head to sniff their fragrance. "Thank you." She spoke so softly he scarcely heard her.

She had not said she accepted his apology, but since she had taken the bouquet, he decided to consider that a tacit acceptance. Best to leave it at that for the nonce, he told himself. Tomorrow he would have more flowers delivered, dozens of roses—pink ones instead of white.

She did not speak again, and he, believing silence on his part might be wise, did not talk either, until he halted the horses before her house. Freddie ran out as he jumped down to help her dismount.

"Miss Ash—Alcida," he said. "Mr. Gounod come by to collect 'is rig. Mad as 'ops, 'e were. Said 'e was sore tempted to call 'is lordship out."

Well aware Liam would never do any such thing,

Damon glanced at Alcida and surprised a tiny smile on her face that showed the charming dimple in her left cheek. "I fear Lord Damon may deserve exactly such a fate," she said.

At least she had not added that she hoped Liam was a crack shot. After seeing her to the door, Damon took her gloved hand and brought it to his lips. "Until next we meet," he said. Turning quickly, he left before she could reply.

Standing in the open door, Ashley watched him drive off. "Rats and mice!" she muttered to Freddie. "He hurried away before I could tell him I never want to see him again."

"Most likely on purpose 'cause 'e didn't want to 'ear it," Freddie told her. " 'E's sweet on ye, 'e is. Anyone can see that."

"That does not signify," she said. "Not to me."

That evening at White's, Damon was a consistent loser, while Liam won. "You have the edge on me," Damon told him.

"In cards, perhaps," Liam replied. "What's the old saying you reminded me of? *Lucky at cards, unlucky at love.* Don't have the edge with Miss Blayne—you do, you sly old fox."

One of Liam's most endearing qualities was his inability to hold a grudge. Damon draped an arm over his shoulder. "Not much of an edge."

"Did I hear Miss Blayne's name?" Lord Haverstall spoke from behind Damon.

Turning, Damon was about to speak when Liam said, "Damon and I are rivals for her attention. Prettiest songbird in London. Or anywhere, I should think."

Haverstall nodded. "Seen her on-stage more than once. Charming voice, lovely smile. The dimple that comes and goes in her right cheek makes a man want to vault onto the stage, swoop her into his arms, and carry her off."

"Left cheek," Damon corrected.

Haverstall shook his head. "Right cheek, old man. I will have you know I am a connoisseur of dimples, facial and otherwise."

"Liam?" Damon said. "Settle this, if you will."

"Thought 'twas the left," Liam said, "but could be I'm confusing her with that rustic gal in Lincolnshire, what's-her-name, the one we mistook for Miss Blayne."

"Miss Ashley Douglas," Damon told him. "True, she did have a dimple in her left cheek. But so does Miss Blayne."

"Right cheek," Haverstall insisted. "Pattson," he called to a friend, "Come over a moment, if you will, and prove Damon wrong."

Pattson was almost certain it was the right cheek. He called to another man for confirmation and soon everyone in White's was involved, leading to wagers on the outcome, with odds favoring the right cheek.

"She's appearing at the Haymarket tomorrow evening," Haverstall announced. "We shall all go and observe."

Damon had no intention of waiting that long. He would call on Alcida in the morning, and for more reasons than the dimple, see her, whether she wished to be home to him or not.

The following day, he waited until he was certain his two dozen pink roses had been delivered before he ventured to knock on her door. Alcida answered the door herself, greeting him so eagerly that he was taken aback.

"I am so pleased to see you, sir," she said. "I was about to have Freddie deliver a note to you. I am at my wit's end and only you can help me."

He smiled at her, elated at the promising turn of events. "Whatever you wish, I shall do."

"I fear I have lost my most precious possession," she said. "Do you recall me wearing a gold locket shaped like a heart?"

He thought a bit and recalled her tugging at some bauble around her neck but could not picture what it had been. "I believe you did wear something depending from a gold chain," he said cautiously.

"My locket!" she cried. "I must find it."

Since they were both still standing in the entry, he said, "Perhaps we could sit down and discuss where you might last have worn the locket."

"I *am* sorry. Do come into the parlor. I fear I am at sixes and sevens over this and have quite lost my manners."

When they were both seated in the tiny parlor, he asked, "When did you last see the locket?"

She glanced away from him. "In—in the mews. I recall having my hand up, holding it, a very bad habit I am prone to. I do not recall touching the locket afterward, and when I retired last night, it was gone. Ursula, Freddie and I have searched the house and the grounds and the street without success."

"You are saying you believe it might be in my curricle?"

She nodded. "I cannot imagine what else could have happened to it."

He was about to rise and suggest they search the rig when Freddie burst into the parlor. " 'Tain't in Lord Damon's curricle, Miss Ash—Alcida, 'cause I looked real good. Found this, sir." He proffered a ruby-headed gold cravat pin of Liam's that had been missing for a fortnight.

Damon pocketed the pin with thanks and insisted Freddie accept a few shillings for his honesty. "Mr. Gounod will like as not offer you a guinea," he said. "The pin was his grandfather's."

"Ain't no sign o' the gold locket, though," Freddie said, after thanking him for the money. "Wish I'd o' found that."

Tears misted Alcida's eyes, making Damon wish they were alone so he could put his arms around her for comfort. There was no denying his strong impulse to protect her from the slings and arrows of the world about her.

"I shall post a reward," he told her, "as well as return immediately to the mews and search there."

"Thank you, you are most kind," she said, her voice quivering. "I would rather have lost all I possess than my locket. My mother gave it to me."

As he remembered, she had spoken only of a foster mother. "Mrs. Blayne?"

She shook her head. "My real mother. I was too young to know her, but she left me the locket. It can never be replaced."

Rising, he said, "I shall do all I can to recover this

heart-shaped locket for you, starting at this moment." He spoke from his own heart, unable to bear
the sight of her woebegone face.

She offered him a pale imitation of her usual smile,
but he caught a brief glimpse of her dimple and it
was, as he had been positive it would be, in her left
cheek.

"I can only pray you are successful," she said.

He stopped by his house before setting off for the
mews, planning to send the reward notice to be
posted. Jenkins, his valet, met him at the door. "I
tried to catch you before you left, sir," he said, "but
you were out the door and gone."

"Yes, what is it?" Damon asked impatiently.

"I found this caught in your jacket, sir. Evidently
the chain broke and the torn link penetrated the
material. I regret that I did not notice it until this
morning." Jenkins held up a broken chain with a
gold heart-shaped locket trapped at the fastener end.

"Good man!" Damon took the locket and chain
from him. "You deserve a bonus for finding this, and
I shall see you receive it."

Jenkins's usually solemn face broke into a gratified
smile. "I was merely doing my job but thank you, sir,
thank you indeed."

"I shall require an appropriate box to return this
in," Damon said, thinking ahead with anticipation to
the warm welcome he would receive from Alcida.

"Right away, sir."

Left alone while Jenkins went off to secure a box,
Damon took the locket into the library, seated himself at the desk, and laid the trinket on the polished
mahogany surface. Heart-shaped it was, but small—

perhaps because it had been made for a child to wear. Alcida had mentioned that she had received the locket when she was too young to remember the occasion. Wondering if it opened, he pried at a tiny crack with his thumbnail. Before it occurred to him that he might be violating Alcida's privacy by looking inside, the two hinged halves parted.

He could not resist glancing into it. He had half-expected a curl of hair or a miniature portrait but the locket contained nothing but an inscription—one word. Seeing the elaborately scrolled A, he assumed the word would be her name. Ready to close it, he held, staring, not believing his own eyes.

Ashley?

Impossible!

Yet he could not doubt the evidence of his own eyes. Why was Alcida wearing a locket, one she treasured, moreover, that had the name Ashley engraved inside? 'Twas not a common name. Of course it could have been her mother's name. Or a family name. On the other hand, the locket had obviously been made for a child; would not it be more logical to place inside the name of the child the locket was intended for?

The only Ashley he had ever met was the lass in Lincolnshire. Ashley Douglas, who looked exactly like Alcida Blayne. One and the same? He shook his head. Aunt Tally had insisted the rustic maiden really was Ashley Douglas, an orphan taken in by a foster family.

Alcida had been raised by a foster mother. Had she also been an orphan? Two orphans, two lockets? Twins? Had their birth mother had the lockets made

with the names inside in order to tell the twins apart?
If so, why was Alcida wearing the locket with Ashley's
name inside?

He had no answers at the moment, but by God, he
meant to find some. Hearing a knock, he absently
said, "Enter." Jenkins came in and laid a red velvet
ring box on the desk.

"Capital," he told the valet. Once Jenkins left the
room, he fell to brooding over the locket once again.

His first impulse, to drive back to Alcida and de-
mand to know what was going on, fell by the wayside.
She might lie or she might honestly not know the
truth and he would not be able to tell the difference.

"Lancaster Hall," he muttered. "The very place.
Ashley Douglas lives in Lincolnshire and I shall enlist
Aunt Tally's aid in ferreting out the truth. The locket
comes with me so Alcida will be forced to mourn her
loss until my return."

Pulling paper from a drawer, he scribbled a note to
the effect that he had been called away and would see
her on his return, saying nothing about the locket.
After signing and sealing it, he asked a footman to
deliver the note, then prepared for the journey.

Aunt Tally was surprised to see him and professed
herself delighted as well.

He had decided on the way to the hall that he
would not reveal everything at once. Not that he
meant to lie to his aunt, but he did not wish to cause
trouble for anyone in case he was making a mountain
out of a molehill.

Waiting until she'd ordered tea, he said as casually

as he could, "Is Miss Douglas still living with the Grahams?"

Aunt Tally blinked, looking startled. "Why, no, dear boy, don't you recall? I am certain I told you Ashley had been hired by our local duke to be his daughter's governess. Ashley is currently living at Humber's Hall."

"You mean Farrington, Duke of Roxton?" he asked. A faint stirring in his memory told him he had heard the news before and that he had not liked the sound of it then any better than he did now.

"Don't know the man well," he muttered, "but Liam once told me there was some funny business about his wife's death."

"Madeline fell off a horse and broke her neck." Aunt Tally spoke flatly. "We all knew she was on her way to Gypsy Grove to visit the band of gypsies camped there at the time. Not to have her fortune told, oh, no. To rendezvous with her latest lover."

Damon raised his eyebrows. "A Rom?"

"Some women of our class apparently become fascinated by gypsy men and seek them out, as you should know. Think of the song *The Raggle-taggle Gypsies, O* and ask yourself why it was written if not because gently bred women are sometimes strangely drawn to the uncouth."

"The duke allowed that demeaning liaison to go on?"

Aunt Tally shrugged. "We prefer to believe he did not know. In any case, the gypsies have never returned to the grove since she died. How did we get onto this depressing subject, anyway? Oh yes, you asked about Ashley." She eyed him shrewdly. "Merely a passing interest, I assume?"

"I don't like to think of her living at Humber's Hall with a man who may have arranged his wife's death."

"And so?"

"I intend to pay her a visit. Surely governesses can have visitors."

Aunt Tally glanced away from him, apparently interested in her white cat, sleeping on a parlor footstool. "I do not believe you should," she said.

"Nevertheless, I am going to."

"You should not bother the young lady. We both know your intentions toward her are not of the best."

"My intentions have nothing to do with my visit. I merely wish to know she is well and not under duress."

"Duress? Good heavens, Charles, what has gotten into you?"

I don't enjoy being duped, if that is what is happening, he thought but did not say. If I am wrong and 'tis merely a mistake, then I don't care to broadcast it.

"Did you not ever hear of rakes reforming?" he asked with a twisted smile.

Aunt Tally cast him a speaking look. "I shall hope the duke takes your visit in good grace and it does not cost Ashley her position there."

"I shall be a perfect model of decorum. In fact, I may well tell the man that you were anxious to know how Ashley was getting on and sent me to inquire."

She smiled disbelievingly. "Tact? From you? Still, I suppose 'tis better belated than never."

"And here I thought I was your favorite nephew."

"I admit that you are in the running, at least most of the time. Since I apparently have not been able to dissuade you from this folly, please do remember to give Ashley my regards."

He nodded. "My cattle need a rest. May I borrow your pair?"

"Of course, though I am surprised you deign to drive an unmatched set. Not to mention slow-paced."

He grinned at her. "Perhaps I shall set a new fashion, think on it."

The sun was setting as he turned into Humber's Harp and negotiated the shadowy drive with vastly overgrown trees and shrubs to either side. "Man needs a new set of gardeners," he muttered.

He had never been to the place before, and when the house came into view, he shook his head as he viewed the moat. What an ancient, gloomy old pile, no doubt as dark inside as out. While he could not approve of Roxton's wife bedding a Rom, he could understand her desire to spend as little time as possible inside Roxton's ancestral halls.

Fortunately the drawbridge appeared to be permanently let down and did not now connect directly to the main entrance of the house. He negotiated it with the curricle, turning off and entering a porte-cochère that was obviously a later addition.

"Miss Ashley Douglas," he told the somber old butler who opened the door to his knock.

There was a moment of silence. "The young lady is not at home, sir," the butler finally said.

"Then I shall come inside and wait until her return."

The butler did not move aside. "If I may suggest,

sir, it would be more convenient for you to come back in about seven days. Miss Douglas is at present, in London with His Grace and Lady Clematis."

"London!"

"Yes, sir. As I mentioned, they should be at home seven days from now."

What the devil was she doing traveling alone with Roxton? Alone except for the child, who was not a proper chaperon.

He thanked the butler, ran down the steps, and climbed into the curricle. What a wild-goose chase. Nothing for it now but to return to the city and run down Ashley there. As he recalled, the Roxton town house was somewhere near Haverstall's place.

"You are going back to London in the morning?" Aunt Tally exclaimed, when he reached the Dower House and sought her out in her favorite place, the morning room. "Why so quickly? You only just arrived."

"Miss Douglas—Ashley—is in London with the evil duke."

"He is not what I consider evil."

"She should not be alone with him, her reputation will be in shreds."

"She is a governess, dear boy. An employee of Roxton's. Do not take on so."

"She is also an innocent girl. God knows what is happening to her."

"In my opinion," Lady Lancaster observed, "that young lady at Humber's Harp is well able to take care of herself."

"She's not there; she's in London. Which is why I am returning posthaste."

"Will you not allow me one small clue as to what is troubling you?"

Damon ran a hand through his hair. " 'Tis complicated."

"Which means you do not wish to tell me anything."

"How can I, when I do not understand what this means." He extracted the red velvet box and dumped its contents in his aunt's lap."

" 'Tis a gold locket," she said, fingering it, "with a broken chain."

"The locket belongs to Alcida—that is, Miss Blayne, the London songstress. 'Twas lost by her, and I happened to find it. Open it, if you will, and examine the inside."

Aunt Tally obeyed. She peered into the locket and murmured, "Ashley."

"Exactly. What I wish to discover is whether Ashley is also in possession of a similar heart-shaped locket, and if so, what the name inscribed in hers may be."

Aunt Tally looked away from him toward her white cat, dozing on a pillow decorating the seat of a rocker. After a long moment, she turned her attention to him once again. "This contretemps promises to become most interesting," she told him. "I do believe I shall travel to London with you."

Fourteen

In London, Roxton, riding past the Haymarket, caught a glimpse of a poster advertising the theater bill and blinked. Was he seeing aright? In the busy street, he was not immediately able to turn his new black gelding, Jupiter, to go back for a second look. When he finally did turn and pass the theater again, he saw he had not been wrong. The artist who drew the picture of "The London Songbird" had depicted an amazing likeness of Ashley Douglas.

The singer's name, he noted, was Miss Alcida Blayne, and she would be appearing the following night. He made up his mind to go and see her perform. Perhaps he would escort Miss Douglas. Alone, since Clematis would be staying with a friend and not be at home to beg to be taken along. 'Twould be Ashley's first glimpse of a London theater performance, and watching a singer who resembled her should add a fillip to their evening out.

He had business in London and had brought Ashley and his daughter with him on the pretext of allowing them to choose their own books for study. Clematis had accused him of not daring to let them out of his sight because he feared they would concoct another perilous adventure while he was gone. The truth was, he could not bear to be parted from Ashley for so much as a day.

She had rendered him so addlepated that 'twould be a wonder if he could conduct any business at all. And he had not even bedded the lass yet. For a country girl, she seemed unusually adept at parrying his every attempt to seduce her. It would, he had promised himself, be different here in London.

At the duke's town house, meanwhile, Alcida sat at a small writing desk near her bedchamber window, putting the finishing touches on her plan to arrange a secret meeting with her twin sister. She dared not send a note from the house for fear a servant would tattle to Thomas. Ever since that night in the tower when he had insisted she call him by his given name when they were alone, she had thought of him as Thomas. At the same time, she had tried very hard never to be alone with him, well aware of what would happen.

Folding the note she had composed, she sealed and stamped it, then secreted it in her reticule and rose. She glanced in the cheval glass as she passed and sighed at her image. How Ashley could tolerate these drab-colored, high-necked gowns was quite beyond her. She intended to purchase enough material while in London to have at least two up-to-the-mark dresses made for herself. Actually, the purchase was part of her plan.

Opening her door, she glanced across the hall and through an open door where Lady Clematis was all but hanging out of one of her bedchamber windows. "Do be careful," she cautioned the girl, as she crossed into her room.

Lady Clematis eased back and turned to look at her. "I declare," she grumbled, "you are becoming more like Papa every day, worrying that I may come to grief when I am perfectly safe."

"I have become very fond of you," Alcida retorted, "and so you must accept the result."

The girl smiled widely and ran across the room to hug her. Alcida hugged her warmly in return, her heart turning over when she heard Lady Clematis whisper, "Please don't ever go away and leave me."

The girl badly needed a mother.

As if hearing Alcida's unspoken thought, Lady Clematis pulled away and closed the door, shutting them into the bedchamber. Taking Alcida's hand, she drew her to the corner where two slipper chairs faced one another. When they were seated, she said, "I was afraid to come to London, you know."

"I realized you were troubled during the journey here," Alcida replied, "though I did not know why."

"And now I am once again going to visit my friend, Helena Larchmont. You will still be here when I return, will you not?"

Alcida smiled reassuringly. "I shall, as you are well aware. Why are you so overset? Your stay at your friend's house is only for two days and nights."

Lady Clematis's voice dropped to a near-whisper. "It reminds me that I was in London on a fortnight's visit to Helena's house when my mother was killed riding Ceres."

Alcida's hand flew to her mouth. She had learned Lady Clematis's mother had died in an accident, but not how.

"Papa blamed the mare and almost put Ceres

down. Cobb saved her, but Papa would never allow anyone to ride her after what had happened." Tears filled the girl's eyes. "How could the accident have been the mare's fault? My mother was afraid of spirited horses and had picked Ceres because she was so gentle and mild. I tried to tell Papa, but he would never discuss anything related to the accident. So I thought maybe if you rode Ceres he would see the mare was not to blame, after all."

Leaning forward, Alcida patted the girl's knee. "I am sorry that you had to lose your mother. I realize how difficult a time you must have had because I, as an orphan, cannot remember my mother. There has always been an empty spot where memories of her should have been."

Lady Clematis burst into tears. Alcida rose and drew the girl to her feet, cuddling her in her arms. "I know, I know," she murmured.

The girl flung herself away from Alcida and onto the bed, sobbing as though her heart would break. Alcida sat next to her, patting her back soothingly.

After a time, Lady Clematis sat up abruptly, and still weeping, said brokenly, "You would not so much as touch me if you knew how evil I am. I hated my mother! She used to tell her friends that she never would have married my father if she had known what an ugly child he would sire. 'Pale as skimmed milk,' I heard her say about me. 'Skinny as a stick, with no-color hair. If he did not possess money and a title, we should never be able to marry her off.' "

Tears stung Alcida's eyes at such cruelty. How could

a mother not love her own child, no matter what she looked like?

"So, you see, my mother never wanted me," the girl added sorrowfully. "How could I love her?"

Alcida moved closer to Lady Clematis, putting an arm around her shoulders and offering her a handkerchief. "My mother abandoned us—that is, me—when I was only three. Yet I think she did love me because she believed that in leaving me she was assuring my future. You see, she had neither money nor husband and then met a man who promised her I would be well taken care of if she left us—me—behind when they moved to France."

Lady Clematis alternated between scrubbing at her wet face with the lace-edged square of white cloth and staring at Alcida. "You don't hate her for leaving you behind?" she demanded.

Alcida shook her head. "I was fortunate enough to be taken in by a foster mother who loved me."

"My mother did not love my father any more than she did me. I used to hear the servants whisper to each other about her meeting other—other men." The girl's voice broke and new tears brightened her eyes.

Alcida gave her shoulders a squeeze. "Your mother is no longer alive and so you must bury your bad memories of her as she is buried because 'tis your memories of her that are bad, not you, yourself. I did not know her so I cannot and shall not pass judgment. But I do know your father and he loves you very much. Do you doubt that?"

The girl blinked back her tears, a tentative smile curving her lips. "Papa does love me. He always has.

He says I look like my grandmother on the Farrington side. I have looked at her picture in the gal-
lery and she is quite beautiful, so I am sure he is
wrong. What do you think?"

"I think you have the distinct possibility of becoming a lovely young lady. I believe it likely your pale
complexion will be much envied, as you mature you
will be graceful and willowy rather than thin, and
admirers will praise your strawberry-blond hair. I
cannot comment on the portrait of your grandmother because, as I have mentioned before, Humber's Harp is so dark 'tis impossible to see anything
clearly."

A tiny giggle escaped the girl. She leaned against
Alcida and murmured, "I love you. I pray you will
stay with me always."

Her heart full, Alcida made the only promise she
honestly could. "I will try."

The rattle of a carriage outside sent Lady Clematis
to her feet. She dashed to the window and announced,
"Their carriage is here and I am not nearly ready!"

"Almost, though," Alcida assured her, ringing the
bell for a maid, then pouring water into the basin so
she could offer the girl a damp cloth to press against
her reddened eyes. "The carriage will wait."

Once she had seen Lady Clematis off, Alcida put
on the one hat of Ashley's that she could tolerate—a
straw bonnet—and drew on gloves. Landis, the butler, had already arranged for the carriage to be
brought around, and so, with a carefully chosen maid
in tow, she was soon rattling along on her way to
Bond Street, ostensibly to go shopping.

Lily, the young maid, was so obviously smitten with

the footman who rode tiger that Alcida anticipated no problems, since the two would be so distracted by one another that what she was up to would escape Lily's notice.

On Bond street, she indicated a drapery shop to the driver. She was not pleased that he had to pull over several shops beyond the one she had indicated because Ashley, looking for a Roxton carriage, might not be certain in which shop she was waiting. Still, if she remained alert, she should be able to spot the "black widow" easily enough.

After alighting, she hurried into the drapery shop, saying to Lily, "Remain with the carriage, if you please." The maid did not argue.

Once inside, Alcida arranged with the proprietor for the note she had written to be delivered, then began examining various bolts of cloth.

Ashley, cast down by the loss of her locket and by Lord Damon's—she would *not* call him Charles, even in her thoughts—apparent defection, was listlessly embroidering a table runner when Ursula brought her in a note that had just been delivered.

"Not from Lord Damon, I'd wager," Ursula said, "because a common street arab delivered it. He's waiting for the answer."

Frowning in puzzlement, Ashley set aside her sewing and examined the folded and sealed paper. She gasped when she recognized the impress on the seal as the Duke of Roxton's. Quickly breaking it, she unfolded the paper and scanned the words.

"Listen," she told Ursula and began to read:

My Dear Sister,
   I am in London. Become the lady in black and meet me on Bond Street. You know whose carriage will be by the shop I am in.

                                                    Your sister

"If you go, you're both taking a chance," Ursula warned.

Moving to the tiny writing desk to pen an answering note, Ashley said, "I shall don that gloomy black costume, complete with veil, and no one will have a clue to my identity. Please call Freddie and have him find me a rig. Oh, Ursula, I am so excited. I have longed to talk to Alcida. 'Tis passing strange that after years of not even knowing I had a twin I should miss her so very much."

Damon, tired from his speedy but fruitless journey to and from Lincolnshire, was further irked by finding no one but the servants at home when he reached the Duke of Roxton's town house. In addition, Jenkins had reminded him of his appointment with his tailor for a final fitting of his new coat and he loathed the tedium of fittings. Since he had time to waste, though, he decided he might as well keep the appointment. He set off for Bond Street in a foul temper.

Roxton, realizing he was near Bond Street, and having noticed on the journey to London that Ashley's gloves were badly worn at the fingertips, decided on impulse to stop and buy her several new pairs. Having held her hand, he thought he could judge her size without too much difficulty. He would say the gloves were a gift from both him and Clematis so she would not refuse.

He longed to give her more, to dress her in the very latest fashion, to shower her with jewels, to offer her everything she wanted—but he shook his head. He knew her well enough by now to understand that until he bedded her and she became his mistress, she would reject all offerings.

Thinking about the night in the tower when he had warmed her feet, he was reminded of the passion he had roused in her—quickly banked, true, but unmistakably there—and lost himself in a reverie of what she would be like in bed with her passion fully unleashed. Absentmindedly he reined in his horse when he came to a likely shop, forgetting he was not riding Zeus, who never flinched at any provocation, but instead, his new London acquisition, the black named Jupiter.

He paid no attention to the hired rig that had pulled up just behind him, nor to the small brindle dog at the curb. Dismounting, he only half-noticed the door to the rig open and a young red-haired footman jump down to assist the woman passenger alight. The boy tripped over the brindle dog and the dog started to yap and then began snapping at everything in sight, including the woman in black who was stepping down from the rig. She screamed.

Jupiter took offense at the noise, rearing back and all but jerking the reins from Roxton's hands. In struggling to control the horse in order to tie him to the post, Roxton stumbled against the woman, who was trying to avoid the dog. Fast footwork enabled him to prevent them both from falling, but in the process, one of his buttons caught in her veil, jerking the veil aside so that her face was exposed.

He gaped. "Ashley!" he exclaimed.

She stared at him in obvious astonishment. "Your Grace!" she stammered.

"What are you doing here?" he asked.

She backed away. "You are making a mistake," she told him.

Certain he was not, he advanced toward her. She held up her hands as though to protect herself, making him say, "You know I shan't hurt you."

"But I am not who you think I am," she wailed.

Damon, coming up Bond Street, saw a man in front of one of the shops who seemed to be threatening a woman dressed in black. Slowing, he took a second look, recognizing the man as Roxton. At that moment the woman in black turned her face toward him and he shouted, "Ashley!

Abandoning his curricle in the street, Damon leaped out and raced to the rescue. By this time Roxton was reaching for her as she cowered away from him. Damon grasped Roxton from the rear, attempting to pin his arms. Roxton fought him like a madman. In the ensuing struggle, the woman in black vanished.

"In here," Alcida ordered, shoving her sister bodily into the drapier's. A uniformed boy she recognized as Freddie followed them inside.

Hurriedly pulling coins from her reticule, without looking at them, Alcida shoved them at the sputtering proprietor and pulled Ashley with her around the counter and into the back room, ordering Freddie to follow. "I saw what happened," she said. "To avoid a disaster, we all must disappear. Quickly, into the alley."

Once they left the drapier's shop through the rear door, Freddie took charge, leading them by a circuitous route onto the next street, where he hailed a hired hack.

Outside the shop, a gathering crowd surrounded Roxton and Damon, enjoying the impromptu fisticuffs. As the two men broke apart to circle one another, Roxton, apparently recognizing Damon for the first time, called his name.

"Damon! Why the bloody hell did you jump me?"

Damon glared at him. "You were attacking Miss Douglas."

"Damned if I was. Merely trying to find out why she was on Bond Street dressed as she was. Left her at home taking care of my daughter."

Damon scowled at him. "Any fool could see she was afraid of you. What have you been doing to her?"

Roxton blinked. "Why, nothing."

"You lie! She was scared out of her wits."

Roxton's face turned brick red. "No man calls me a liar." He whipped off his gloves and slapped Damon lightly across the cheek. "Name your second, sir."

Damon drew himself up and made a curt bow. "Very well. He will call on you to set a time and place."

That settled, both men turned as one to look for

Ashley. She was nowhere in sight and none of the bystanders, who were rapidly dispersing, would admit to seeing her disappear. Damon watched Roxton accost a uniformed man he took to be the duke's servant, then followed the two men to a carriage bearing the Roxton coat of arms on the door. When he was satisfied that only a fearful young maid was inside, he strode off.

An hour later, his search for Ashley having proved fruitless, Damon returned home. His aunt, who had ridden to London with him and slept late, was outside, looking over his front garden, when he arrived. She listened to his recounting of the event on Bond Street.

"Reduced to brawling on the streets, now, are you?" she asked, her eyebrows raised.

"The outcome was that Roxton challenged me to a duel," he finished.

Aunt Tally clutched at her chest. "Good Lord above!"

"I had no choice but to accept," he added.

"You have no idea how wrong you are," she said. "The both of you. What a dreadful coil this has become. Help me into the house and send a note 'round to His Grace that Lady Lancaster demands an immediate interview with him. Once I sit down and catch my breath, I shall endeavor to order my thoughts so that when he arrives I shall be able to make my explanation coherent."

An hour later, tight-lipped and wearing a formidable scowl, the duke arrived. At Lady Lancaster's insistence, he seated himself with the air of a man whose time is being wasted. He did not so much as glance at Damon.

"I trust Miss Douglas arrived at your home safely," she said to him.

"She is home," he admitted.

"I thought she would be, since she is most resourceful. Far more so than the actual Miss Ashley Douglas."

Both men stared at her as though she had mislaid her wits. She smiled a bit guiltily at first one, then the other. "When I proposed this masquerade, I had no inkling it would eventually cause a duel between the two of you. You will soon see that there is no reason for you to be at odds. The fault, I fully admit, lies with me."

"I do not understand one word you have said." The duke's tone indicated he believed what she'd told him to be total clap-twaddle.

Damon, poised to agree with Roxton, paused as the oddity of the name in the locket struck him anew. "Masquerade, Aunt Tally?" he asked. "What exactly do you mean?"

"Simply put, not one but two young women are involved. Identical twins, who only last month discovered each other's existence. One, of course, is Ashley Douglas, the other is Miss Alcida Blayne."

Despite the inscription he'd found in the locket, Damon was shaken. Roxton appeared to be completely dumbfounded. "I know I hired Ashley as my daughter's governess," he insisted.

Lady Lancaster shook her head. "You believed you had. The young lady who came to Humber's Harp was and is actually Alcida Blayne."

"But why, in God's name?" Roxton pleaded.

"Quite frankly, your gossip-fed sinister reputation frightened poor Ashley into believing you were some kind of ogre. She desperately wished to refuse your offer, but her foster family insisted she take the position. Alcida, on the other hand, was not a bit afraid of you, and her more worldly experience suggested to me that she was more capable than her sister of dealing with whatever conditions prevailed at Humber's Harp.

"Since Ashley sings as well as her sister does, it appeared to me to be quite natural to suggest they switch roles. To go back a bit, they will be coming into quite a decent little inheritance when they turn twenty-one, so the masquerade would only have encompassed the two years until then."

"How in the devil did you get mixed up with the situation in the first place?" Damon asked.

She told them about Alcida's illness and Ashley's frantic plea for help in treating her newfound sister. "We prevented immediate discovery," she said, "by having Ashley dress in black and wear a black veil the way her sister had done when she arrived at the inn in Louth. Thus Alcida became Ashley during her illness at my place and Ashley became the unknown lady in black, later traveling in that disguise to London with Freddie, the Grahams' former stableboy, as her groom.

"Naturally, she carried a note from Alcida to her companion, Ursula, explaining the turn of events. Up until now, everything has gone smoothly."

Damon eyed his aunt assessingly, a plan forming in his mind. "So besides the twin sisters, only you,

Ursula, and Freddie are aware of the switch—or even the twinship."

"That is correct," she told him, "though, of course, my butler, Langdon, did assist us. He will not give the secret away."

Damon glanced at Roxton, who continued to appear stunned. "Do you still care to pursue the duel, sir?" he inquired.

Roxton waved a hand. "No reason to, under the circumstances. We were equally fooled."

"May I make a proposal?" Damon asked him.

"Fire away."

Turning a severe gaze on his aunt, Damon said, "This will depend on Lady Lancaster's being able to keep quiet about letting us in on the masquerade."

"I know how to keep my mummer dubbed," she said, straight-faced, taking both men aback.

Damon recovered first. "I take it you have been exposed to Freddie."

She smiled. "Bright lad. He will go far."

Turning to Roxton, Damon said, "How do you feel about keeping the secret a secret, at least for a time? That is, not tell Alcida or Ashley that we are on to them."

Roxton smiled slightly. "I should enjoy paying them back in their own coin. Brilliant of you, Damon." He rose and bowed to Lady Lancaster. "I thank you for not condemning me as so many have done. Gossip can be as vicious as a mad dog."

She nodded. "My husband believed you were a good man, and he was a most excellent judge of people."

"I feel I must tell you," he said, "that Miss

Douglas—that is, Miss Blayne—has exposed the Humber's Harp ghost as a natural phenomenon, the action of a strong wind producing enough power to sound the harp strings. As you suspected, she is an unusual woman. I bid you adieu, Lady Lancaster."

Damon, who had risen with Roxton, walked with him to the door and then exited with him. "Another thought has occurred to me," he said, pausing before they reached the duke's carriage. "I have the notion that uncovering the kinship between these two young women is but the tip of an iceberg. Mysteries intrigue me, and I fancy a look into the twins' ancestry. Would you care to assist me?"

"A capital idea," Roxton said, clapping him on the shoulder. "I shall discreetly question Miss Blayne. You might begin with your esteemed, though admittedly devious, aunt. I would wager she knows more secrets than we two could count, and perhaps one of them might bear fruit."

"I shall do that. One more question, if you don't mind. Ashley has a dimple in her left cheek—does Miss Blayne, by any chance, have a dimple in her right cheek?"

Roxton thought a moment before nodding. "So she does."

Another riddle solved, Damon told himself. If he and Roxton had not parted friends, at least they were on reasonably good terms. He watched the carriage roll away, relieved that the duel had been aborted—he had not wished to injure Roxton.

Aunt Tally's revelations had also solved the dimple question, not to mention the locket inscription. Who would have expected a little country miss to carry off such a successful masquerade? Ashley had convinced everyone who mattered that she really *was* the London songbird she pretended to be.

Was I ever truly convinced? he asked himself. In the depths of my heart did I not know I was entranced here in London with the same sweet but spirited girl I had already met in Lincolnshire?

He could not be sure. One thing *was* clear to him, though. Aunt Tally might not have raised even one eyebrow if he had successfully managed a liaison with Alcida Blayne. But she would never forgive him if he made Ashley Douglas his mistress.

Fifteen

Four days later, seated in Damon's library, Roxton and Damon compared notes.

"I tried to be cautious when questioning Alcida about her background," Roxton said, "but I have never been accounted a tactful man. I believe she sensed a change in my attitude. I realize she had to decide whether to give me what Ashley might know or her own recollections, so I cannot be certain which she settled for. She told me she had heard 'somewhere' that her mother's maiden name was Winfield. Alice Winfield."

"The name Winfield is familiar, though I cannot immediately place it," Damon said.

"Old family from the Lakes Region. No one left except an elderly grandfather, or so others have told me. But the name triggered a memory from my childhood, an old scandal I overheard my parents discussing. As nearly as I can recall, the granddaughter, who was somewhat older than my mother, ran off, supposedly with a tutor. The tutor, subsequently located, swore he had had nothing to do with her disappearance. His wife said the same. The strange circumstances intrigued my mother."

"Was the daughter ever found?"

"I have no idea. I shall pursue the matter further."

"Aunt Tally had nothing useful for us, but perhaps she can help us with this new revelation, since her mother grew up in the Lakes Region. Let me invite her to join us and we shall ask her about the Winfields."

Not long afterward, he escorted Lady Lancaster in. She greeted the duke politely before seating herself. As soon as the men sat down, she said, "I assume you both intend to pick my brain, but I assure you I know nothing of Ashley's antecedents. She was abandoned at the Methodist orphanage as a wee child and not even the minister had any notion of where she came from."

"Roxton has discovered, from Alcida, the maiden name of the twins' mother," Damon said. " 'Twas Winfield."

Aunt Tally grew animated. "If you mean the Winfields from the Lake Region, my mother often spoke of the family tragedy. She was the same age as their son and had an early *tendresse* for him which she apparently outgrew. In any case, he married an heiress and was rumored to mistreat her. The poor young woman must have had reason to be unhappy, because she drowned herself in a quarry pond shortly after her daughter, the only child of the union, was born.

"Let me see if I can recall the baby's name, something fanciful, I believe, some kind of flower." She frowned, putting a hand to her forehead. After a long pause she crowed triumphantly, "Alyssum, that is the name. Alyssum. Her birthday was the same month and day as mine, though two years later."

Damon glanced at Roxton. Alice could well have been an abbreviated form of Alyssum.

Roxton gave him a brief nod before asking Lady Lancaster, "Do you have any idea what became of Alyssum Winfield?"

Lady Lancaster shook her head regretfully. "All I can tell you is that I never heard her name among those who of us who came out, nor did I ever meet her during a London season. So actually, I never knew her at all."

"She disappeared from home when she was in her late twenties," Roxton said.

"An intriguing mystery, to be sure," Lady Lancaster said. "I shall call upon a few old acquaintances here in London and try to dig up any ancient gossip that may pertain to the matter."

Two days later, the three met again at Damon's town house. "I return to Humber's Harp on the morrow," Roxton said. "I left estate matters pending that must be addressed. Though I cannot put my finger on it, I am sure Alcida suspects something, quite possibly because I did not chide her about the Bond Street episode. To own the truth, I was so troubled by having the masquerade revealed to me that I did not know whether I should pretend that I believed the woman in black was she, as I actually did at the time, or to ignore the matter. In the end, I said nothing."

"We shall continue to nose around here," Damon said, "and will let you know what transpires. Aunt Tally does have one tidbit to share with us."

"I happened to recall that Liam's mother spent part of her short first marriage in the Lake Country," she told them. "That husband, as you may know, was carried off by a fever; subsequently she returned to London, where she met and married Mr. Gounod. Anyway, I visited her. Alyssum Winfield, she said, was never involved with the tutor. The local families suspected she eloped with a visitor to the area, a passing stranger who somehow charmed her reticence away. Though very pretty, Alyssum was apparently painfully shy. I asked, but it was clear no one had ever offered a name to put to the stranger."

"Have you questioned Ashley at all?" Roxton asked Damon.

"He has not called on her since the contretemps on Bond Street," Lady Lancaster put in.

Roxton raised an eyebrow.

" 'Tis the locket," Damon explained. "If I return it I must lie and claim I did not open it, but will she believe me? If I visit and do not mention recovering the locket, that constitutes a lie by omission. My aunt always finds me out when I skirt the truth."

"I have been acquainted with you, young man, since you were in skirts," Lady Lancaster told Damon. "Ashley has not. In my opinion you are afraid to face her, knowing she is not Alcida."

Though he refused to admit she had struck a sore spot, he felt forced to cover himself by announcing he would call on Ashley this very afternoon.

At home, Ashley had given up even the pretense of sewing and was attempting to read a slim volume of Lord Byron's poetry, but he rambled on so that her mind strayed, making her forget to turn the pages. Immediately after the debacle on Bond Street,

she had expected instantaneous exposure of their
scheme, even though Alcida had assured her that neither man had seen them slip away. She had not heard
from Alcida since, so presumably the duke had accepted whatever story Alcida had told him and had
not realized there was a masquerade.

So there was a good chance Lord Damon also had
been fooled, exactly as her sister had said. But if so,
why had he neither called nor sent round a note?
Evidently he had not found her lost locket, because
if he had, surely he would have returned it to her.

She sighed and concentrated once again on the
book, her gaze falling upon these lines:

> Alas! the love of women! it is known
> To be a lovely and a fearful thing
> For all of theirs upon that die is thrown
> And if 'tis lost, life hath no more to bring . . .

Instantly she forgave Lord Byron for the long, dull
poems preceding these four lines. He had written
truly, from the heart; he had written truth.

The truth for her was that she loved Charles Jordon, Marquess of Damon. Why, of all the men in
England, she had chosen him was a mystery she was
unable to solve. She loved a man she could never
wed, a man who cared naught for her, even if he had
proposed she become his mistress because he wanted
her.

Ursula's sad story had illustrated the difference between wanting and loving. Loving did not resort to
trickery, to lies and—Ashley put a hand to her mouth
as a startling thought rattled her. Had she not lied

to Lord Damon? Had she not tricked him? And yet, did she not love him?

Freddie burst into the room, distracting her from her sad pensiveness. " 'E's coming, 'e is," he said excitedly. "Was up to the corner nattering with old Chestnut Pete, I was, 'n' I seen them blacks o' 'is pulling that there fat curricle, so I runs 'ome quick to tell ye."

"Thank you, Freddie." She heard her calm tone with astonishment because her heart was thundering inside her chest and she could scarce draw a full breath.

He nipped out as Ursula entered. "I heard Freddie," she said. "Are you at home to callers?"

Ashley nodded, no longer trusting her voice. How could she turn him away when she wished to see him so very much?

Some minutes later Lord Damon—would she ever be able to think of him as Charles?—entered the parlor rather hesitantly for him. He advanced toward her, carrying what appeared to be a small box on the palm of his right hand, and when he was close enough, he offered it to her.

"The lost has been found," he announced.

Ashley opened the lid of the red velvet box. Nestling inside was her locket, complete with the gold chain. She exclaimed with delight, removing the locket and holding it to her lips.

"I took the liberty of having the chain's broken link repaired," he told her.

"How kind. And how wonderful of you to have found my dearest possession. I can never thank you enough. Where was it?"

"Actually, my valet discovered it attached to the jacket I wore on the day you lost the locket. He did not happen to notice it when he put the jacket away, and I did not happen to wear the jacket for several days, hence the delay."

"You will tell your man how grateful I am?"

"I have already rewarded him, but I shall add your thanks. I believe you told me your birth mother gave you the locket?"

"Yes," she said, wondering why he was asking. It had crossed her mind more than once that if he found the locket, he might well open it. Had he done so? Was that what had prompted the question?

"Do not think me impertinent, but I am curious to know if you ever learned anything about her," he added.

About to say no, Ashley recalled that she was supposed to be Alcida, who did know more about their mother than she. "Count Roulais, the man who rescued mother from poverty and took her to France, visited me a few years ago. You must realize I was left behind at three years of age because the count did not wish to be burdened with children.

"After Mother died, he came to see me and said he was leaving me a legacy in his will to be given to me when I was twenty-one. He has since died. So you see, I must sing for my supper for two more years."

"This French count did not offer any personal information about your mother?"

Ashley tried to remember if Alcida had told her anything else. "Only that her maiden name had been Winfield," she said finally. "Alice Winfield. He said she had consistently refused to discuss her life before they met."

Lord Damon nodded, almost as though he already knew. He could not, of course.

When he remained in what seemed to be a thoughtful silence, she decided to bring up the Bond Street affair, aware she could only do so as gossip she had heard because as far as he knew she had not been present. "I trust you have quite recovered from your bout of fisticuffs with the Duke of Roxton on Bond Street," she said.

"In the event, we wound up settling the matter amicably, so neither he nor I suffered overmuch."

"I am happy to hear that."

He smiled thinly. "Thank you. So am I. I do not believe I mentioned that my aunt, Lady Lancaster, is visiting me here in London. She mentioned that she would enjoy meeting you, as she has never known anyone who performed on the stage. Would it be too much of an imposition if she came to call?"

Ashley, thrilled to hear Lady Lancaster was in London, for she would have news from Lincolnshire, said enthusiastically, "I should be pleased to have Lady Lancaster visit."

"How generous of you. I shall tell her."

Ashley eyed him quizzically. Why was he so stiff today? His demeanor was much more formal than before. Was it because she had turned down his offer to be his fancy woman?

"I shan't keep you," he said, "for I know you have a performance tonight and no doubt wish to rest."

Having no other choice—she did have to perform and she should rest—she nodded politely, waiting for him to ask if he might call on the morrow. Instead, he bowed and said, "Farewell, my dear Miss Blayne."

She murmured her farewell, adding once more that she was grateful for the return of her locket, all the time aware something was wrong between them. She watched him stride from the room and wondered if she would ever see him again.

The evening's performance went well enough but left her exhausted. How did her sister go on with this night after night, week after week? Once in bed, though, she could not dislodge Lord Damon from her thoughts, with the result that sleep eluded her until near morning.

Because she had then slept late, she was scarce dressed when Lady Lancaster sent in her card at two the following afternoon. The older woman bustled into the tiny parlor and embraced Ashley, saying, "My dear, I am so glad to see you."

"How wonderful of you to call," Ashley said. "I assume you know my sister and I tried to meet the other day and succeeded in creating a terrible coil."

"On Bond Street, I believe?"

Ashley rolled her eyes. "I fear the incident is all over town. I am very sorry Lord Damon became mixed up in it."

"He was always impulsive."

"I do believe he is angry with me, though it cannot be over the incident because he would not know I was there."

Lady Lancaster frowned. "Why should he be angry? What leads you to believe he is?"

"I don't know, 'tis just that he behaves differently toward me since then." A thought struck her—she could ask Lady Lancaster, without offense, what she could not ask Lord Damon. "Perhaps you have heard that he found my heart-shaped locket after I lost it. 'Twas exactly like Alcida's, except for the name inscribed inside. You don't suppose he opened it and looked at the name, do you?"

"A *gentleman* would not."

Ashley eyed her in puzzlement. Was she imagining that Lady Lancaster had stressed the word "gentleman" as though to suggest her nephew might not always be one?

"I was wondering, my dear, if I remember correctly," Lady Lancaster said. "I seem to recall that you and your sister mentioned coming into money when you reached twenty-one. Did this information come from a solicitor?"

"Alcida said so. A man in London. I don't believe she told me his name."

"I am asking because I wished to be certain he was a reputable person and not one who might defraud you. It does happen, you know."

"That had not occurred to me," Ashley said. "You might visit Alcida and ask her about him when you return to Lancaster Hall. Have you seen her or spoken to her recently? We did not have a chance to exchange more than a few words at our fateful meeting in Bond Street."

"I have not visited her, but I am returning home in a day or two and shall call on her then. After I do I shall contrive to let you know how she fares."

"What news from Louth? How are the Grahams?"

Lady Lancaster told her all she had heard about

heir Lincolnshire neighborhood, afterward refusing
o stay to tea, pleading another engagement.

When she had left, Ursula joined Ashley for their
afternoon tea. "I have the feeling Lady Lancaster was
rying to tell me something without putting it into
vords," Ashley said.

"Then it must concern her nephew."

"Why do you say that?"

Ursula shrugged. "Who else would she feel loyalty
o but her kin? She would not betray him outright,
out perhaps she believes you need to be warned."

Ashley blinked. "Warned? About what?"

"If I had any idea, I should certainly tell you immediately. How did your conversation with Lady Lancaster go?"

"She passed on local Lincolnshire gossip and
asked a few questions about the solicitor who is han-
lling our legacy from the count. Oh, and I asked her
f she thought her nephew might have opened the
ocket and looked inside. She said a gentleman would
not, but she said it oddly."

"Why would she wish to know about the solicitor?"

"She said she worried about us being defrauded."

"That does happen, but there is no need to worry,
ince Alcida told me your solicitor had a spotless
eputation. If you asked me to wager, I would put my
money on the locket. Gentleman or not, who could
esist looking inside? You can be quite sure he did."

"If he did, he saw my real name. But he did not
ay a word about it."

"To do so means he would have to admit peeking
nside. Do you believe a high-in-the-instep gentleman

is going to be caught out behaving like a man from the common herd?"

"But even if he saw my name and connected it to Lincolnshire, Charles could not possibly know there are two of us."

Ursula raised an eyebrow. "Charles now, is it?"

Ashley blushed. What a time for his given name to slip out!

"Whatever you call the gentleman," Ursula went on, "consider that he may know the impossible and be concealing his knowledge from you. After all, his aunt is aware of the masquerade."

" 'Twas her idea in the first place!" Ashley cried. "She would not give us away."

Ursula gave her a speaking look. "Blood always has been and always will be thicker than water."

Several days later, at Humber's Harp, Hancock brought Lady Lancaster's card in on a silver salver to Alcida, who was in the library with Lady Clematis, the two of them endeavoring to locate Arabia on the globe.

"Lady Lancaster," Alcida said, as she glanced at the card. "How kind of her to call. Would you please show her in here, Hancock?"

"I shall be in the stables while you visit," Lady Clematis told her. "Electra is in need of my attention. Perhaps we can go riding later?"

"Very likely," Alcida agreed. "I shall look for you there."

Lady Lancaster entered the library slowly, watching her step. "How dark this place is," she said. "Whyever does the duke not trim his shrubbery? Forgive my complaints, my dear, but those of us at a certain age come to appreciate a well-lit house."

"The gloom is remarkable," Alcida agreed. "I am so pleased to see you that you may complain all you wish. Do be seated."

Once she was ensconced in a leather chair, Lady Lancaster said, "I cannot think why men insist on leather, but that is my last complaint. I regret that I cannot stay more than a few minutes because my presence is absolutely necessary at the July fête planning meeting and I must be there lest they try to move the site again while I am not on hand to keep the site where it belongs."

She lowered her voice. "I recently called upon your sister in London—I was visiting my nephew during the Bond Street trouble, as you may not be aware. In any case, Ashley is most anxious to know how you are here."

Alcida pitched her voice equally low. "How is she?"

"In excellent health. We were discussing the legacy you both will receive in two years' time, and I may have alarmed her by mentioning that not all solicitors are to be trusted. She was overset since she did not know the man's name."

"Mr. Timothy Jamison is perfectly trustworthy; she need not worry."

Lady Lancaster nodded. "I shall so inform her. How does it go with you? Has the duke proved to be a problem?"

Alcida took a deep breath and let it out slowly. "He is a most misunderstood man," she said. "For a time we seemed to be getting on well, but then, perhaps

because I made it clear I was a governess, not a po
tential mistress, he has become withdrawn." She
leaned forward "I worry about him."

"Goodness me. When did you notice this change?"

"In London. Shortly after he mistook my sister for
me on Bond Street. Actually, she *was* Ashley—but you
know what I mean."

"I am beginning to wonder if I should not have
pruned away my clever plan before it came to frui
tion," Lady Lancaster said. "What did he say about
the Bond Street affair?"

"Not one word. I am reluctant to bring up the sub
ject for fear he suspects more than I realize. The situ
ation makes me uneasy. Does he suspect, and if so
what?"

"Why not mention to him that I discussed the hap
pening at this visit? There would be no need to be
specific as to what we said."

Alcida smiled at her. "You are so very clever."

Lady Lancaster sighed. "Devious is the word less
kind people have used on occasion. One caution
Ashley lost the locket with her name inscribed inside
and 'twas found by my nephew and returned to her
Did he look inside? No one knows, but I think she
suspects he may have. Like the duke to you, Lord
Damon has said nothing to her about it, but she told
me his behavior toward her has changed."

"I am so glad you told me. 'Tis possible we are not
so clever as we have imagined."

Lady Lancaster nodded. "Anything is possible
within this tangled web we have woven." Struggling
up from the deep chair, she added, "I must take my
leave, dear girl. I am pleased you have come to ur

lerstand that Thomas Farrington is no monster. Do
you know he told my nephew that you had banished
the ghost of John Humber?"

"Told your nephew? During the one glimpse I had
of them on Bond Street, he and Lord Damon were
at each other's throats. I assumed they would remain
bitter enemies."

"They settled the problem differently once they
recognized each other," Lady Lancaster said with a
wry smile. "Apparently they have much in common.
And now I really must go."

Alcida walked to the door with her rather than
ringing for Hancock and then let her out herself. At
the last moment, Lady Lancaster patted her hand,
leaned close, and whispered, "Try to be kind to him,
no matter what."

Alcida stood in the doorway staring after her as
her driver helped her into the elderly landau. She
watched the creaky vehicle lumber along the drive
toward the drawbridge, all the time wondering what
on earth Lady Lancaster had meant by her final cryp-
tic remark.

She pondered the question during her ride with
Lady Clematis, evoking a comment from the girl
about how quiet she was.

" 'Tis Papa, is it not?" the girl asked.

Alcida gave her a startled glance. "What do you
mean?"

"I do believe you are worried about him, too. I am
sure you, like I, have noticed the change in him since
we were in London. After you came to Humber's
Harp, he changed for the better, laughing and teas-

ing you. I could tell he liked you, and I was so glad
But now he is slipping back into his old ways."

"Old ways?" Alcida repeated, to gain time to form
some kind of response.

"He is acting much as he did after my mother wa
killed. He was not sad, exactly—I think he must have
known she did not love him. But until you came, he
refused to see anyone except me and his estate man
ager and the servants. He did not behave in that wa
before Mother was killed, so I realize her death af
fected him. He told me once he felt guilty, but I neve
understood why. She was riding alone. How could he
have prevented her fall?"

"I *have* noticed a change in your father," Alcida
said, deciding to be at least partially honest. "I don'
know what caused this change, but I shall endeavo
to find out."

"I think the cause may lie in London," the gir
added.

"Possibly." Not wishing to discuss Thomas furthe
at the moment, Alcida changed the subject, pointing
toward a vine with white flowers twining about an ol
fence post. "Look, is not that plant one we have no
seen before?"

Lady Clematis agreed that it was, so they dis
mounted and took a closer look at the flowers and
leaves. "I do believe I saw a picture of that plant in
our new wildflower book," Alcida said. "I think it i
called traveler's joy. I remember it because the boo
referred to the plant as 'a twiner also known as wil
clematis,' and so I thought of you." She smiled at th
girl.

"You must show me when we get back," Lad

Clematis said excitedly. "I did not know clematis grew wild. Traveller's joy—what a pretty name. I shall ketch it."

When she finished, they remounted and the only conversation on the return ride concerned wildflowers.

After the evening meal, Lady Clematis excused herself, saying she was engrossed in one of the new books bought in London and wished to retire to her bedchamber to read. Alcida understood it might well be the girl's ploy to leave her alone with Thomas. Not, of course, for romantic purposes, but to try to bring him out of his "old ways."

Seeing that he was about to make some excuse to leave her by herself, Alcida confronted him with, "Lady Lancaster was here today. I think we must have a talk."

He looked somewhat taken aback. "Talk?"

Alcida plunged ahead. "Shall we sit in the parlor, or do you prefer the library?"

He shrugged. "You choose."

"The library, I think, for its leather chairs."

Thomas appeared downright puzzled at that remark, and she did not deign to enlighten him.

She sank into the same chair Lady Lancaster had disliked and Thomas seated himself in one opposite hers. "I understand from Lady Lancaster," she began, "that what happened on Bond Street is the latest on-dit in London. She also tells me you and Lord Damon settled the matter amicably. I am sorry to have caused a fuss but relieved to know you and her nephew are not at swords' points." There, she thought, let him try to ignore that.

He did not reply for some time, staring at his boot instead of looking at her. "I suppose," he said at last "that it is true you were at least half the cause of the fuss. Beyond that, I do not care to discuss the matter I have had more than enough of disloyalty in my life Miss Ashley Douglas." The name lashed out at her like the crack of a whip.

He rose and, without so much as a glance at her strode from the room.

Sixteen

"I cannot bear one more hour in London," Ashley told Ursula, as they rode home in the hired rig from her final performance at the Haymarket. "I must get away."

"Where will you go?" Ursula, as usual, remained practical.

"To Lincolnshire. If you agree to accompany me, we can stay at the Harp and Whistle in Louth for a few days."

"You will be recognized and give away the masquerade."

"Not if I arrive as the mysterious lady in black, the way Alcida did."

"She caught some kind of fever there, didn't she? I begged her not to go without me, but she insisted she meant to do things her way. I will say one thing for you, Ashley: you are not quite so stubborn as your sister. I do not approve of the idea, but if you are bent on going, I shall be happy to go with you. I should like to be told why we must visit Lincolnshire, though."

"Because that is my home, and like a sick dog, I want to be in a familiar place," Ashley told her. "I am sick at heart because he knows."

"I assume you refer to Lord Damon and that what he knows is who you actually are. Why are you so sure?"

"It came to me while I was singing tonight, singing a song about lads and maidens gamboling on the green and how the lads are ever playing games while the girls believe in true love."

"I fail to see any connection."

"I love Charles, but I was the one who played the false game. He may not love me, but he was honest all along, even when he asked me to become his mistress. Then he suddenly changed. Not because I refused his offer—I am sure he believed he could convince me in time. No, just as Lady Lancaster was trying to warn me with her veiled hints, Charles changed because he somehow discovered I was not Alcida Blayne but Ashley Douglas, the same girl he had met before, along Dane's Run. He realized I was dishonest, and so he no longer wants me." Her voice broke on the last few words and she began to weep.

"I shall trade places with my sister," she said between sobs, "and live at Humber's Harp. I am no longer afraid of any man, including the duke. She can return to London and the stage, where she belongs."

Ursula put am arm around her. "Don't cry; we will go, if you wish. But let us go openly and honestly, not disguised in black veils."

Ashley's sobbing lessened as Ursula's words penetrated her misery. Yes, she thought, she was finished with masquerading. She would return as who she was. As Ashley Douglas.

* * *

Damon could no longer tolerate the usual rounds in London. Winning at White's was no thrill, bidding for and acquiring the finest horseflesh in England at Tattersall's no longer appealed to him. As for women—he had enough of the fair sex for the nonce. Lounging in his library, with a snifter of French brandy in his hand and more of the liquor warming his stomach, he decided he must get away.

Not to his estate in Kent. He wanted to be coddled, not be depended upon to make decisions. And not to some alien clime where he would be among strangers. Lancaster Hall was the place, he told himself. Aunt Tally would coddle him and he would be in familiar surroundings where no one would expect anything from him and he would be free to do as he wished. Which might very well turn out to be nothing.

"Running away," Liam had called it. Perhaps he was. Damn it, he loved her still, despite her duplicity. In fact, he rather admired the way she had carried it off. Ashley was certainly not the simple rustic maiden he had believed her to be. He had the feeling she would continue to surprise him all his life if he gave her the chance, and he knew he would enjoy it. She was like none other.

Whatever the real Alcida was like, she would not be able to hold a candle to her twin sister.

Hearing a tap at the door, he bade the butler enter. "His Grace, the Duke of Roxton, to see you, Milord," the man said.

Damon sat up straighter. "Show him in, by all means."

Roxton entered and stood staring at the brandy bottle like a man dying of thirst. Or of some other malady, Damon told himself, perhaps the same one affecting me. A woman I want but cannot have.

When Roxton was settled in a chair with his own snifter of brandy, he sighed. "I cannot bear dishonesty," he muttered. "Madeline was the most treacherous woman I ever met. I cannot tolerate another."

"Madeline," Damon repeated. "Your wife, I take it? Never met her."

"If you had, she would have bedded you."

"Worst kind of dishonest," Damon said, vaguely aware the brandy was affecting his discretion, encouraging him to say things he quite possibly should not. The hell with it.

"Last one was a bloody Rom," Roxton went on. "By then, who cared what or who the man was—she was the one I wished dead, and I told her so. A fortnight later her mare threw her on her way to her gypsy lover. Broke her neck. Nearly put down the poor damn mare for doing what I didn't have the courage to do." His laugh was without humor. "Took old Cobb, another bloody Rom, to bring me to my senses. He saved the mare."

"How long ago?" Damon asked.

"Three years."

"Over and done with then. Bury it."

"Did. But she's the same."

Roxton had lost him. "Who?" Damon asked.

"Alcida, or whatever her name is." Roxton poured more brandy into the snifter. "Not an honest bone in her body, but can't put her out of my mind."

"Love her, do you?"

Roxton scowled at him, finally muttering, "So I do. Can't help myself."

Damon chuckled. "In the same boat, both of us. The sisters hooked us and reeled us in. We're flopping around like the foolish fish we are, but we can't get loose."

"Foolish fish. Hard to say. That's us, though."

Damon wondered if he was slurring his words as badly as Roxton. "Fisool fosh," he said.

Roxton laughed. "Told you it was hard. Foosal fiss."

Damon's next attempt was even further off. They both roared with laughter and poured more brandy.

Roxton arrived at Humber's Hall two days later, still feeling slightly under the weather. He half-smiled, remembering the night spent drinking brandy with Damon. Rotten as he had felt the following morning, that night had been worth it. Somehow the binge had cleared his head. He had awakened in one of Damon's guest bedchambers, not at all certain how he had gotten there, but fully aware of what he meant to do about Alcida.

Sometime during the night he had come to realize she was not like Madeline, that her pretense of being her sister was because she was trying to save the poor innocent from the ogre in the castle. From him. She had assumed her twin's identity out of love and had betrayed no one. How could he not admire a woman like that? Admire and love her. He did not care a fig where she came from or who her antecedents were, he intended to marry the wench for good and all. And afterward, he would light every blasted lamp and candle in the house and keep them lit day and night.

Hancock opened the door for him. As he entered,

Clematis darted toward him like a benighted chick and flung herself into his arms. "You drove her away, Papa," she sobbed. "She told me she loved you but she had done you a wrong and so she must leave. I don't know where she has gone."

"Do you mean Alcida is gone?"

Clematis drew back to look into his face. "You called her Alcida! Then you *do* know. She told me all about how she and her twin sister had changed roles, then she said you had found out and you hated her. Please don't hate her, Papa."

"Hate her? I love her as much as you do!"

Clematis's sobs stopped abruptly. "If you love her, you must find her Papa."

"Where was she going?"

"I don't know," Clematis wailed.

Hancock, still standing by the door, cleared his throat. "Excuse me, Milord, but I don't believe the young lady has left the house, because her maid reports that her clothes are still in her room. However, I regret to say we have not been able to find her."

"You searched the house?"

"We did, Milord, at Lady Clematis's request. And the stables. No horse is missing."

Roxton looked at his daughter. "Where did you last see her, Clematis?"

The girl paused in mopping her wet face. "She said she was going to her room to pack her things. I know she really did go there 'cause I followed her, begging her to stay. She would not allow me inside, though."

"Did you or anyone see her come out of her room?"

Clematis shook her head.

Hancock said, "Janet, her maid, insists Miss Douglas never did come out, Milord. But I personally searched the room and she is not there."

"I shall take a look," Roxton said.

Clematis followed him up the stairs and along the gloomy hallway. He had never before actually noticed how ill-lit the corridors were. No wonder Alcida had complained. The door to the bedchamber she had used stood ajar.

"Her door does not stay latched, Papa," his daughter said.

He adored the girl, but having her at his heels under the present conditions annoyed him. He desperately needed to be alone. Aware that to order her to stay in her room would hurt her feelings, he took another tack. Halting and placing his hands on her shoulders, he said, "Clematis, I would like you to do something for me."

"Anything, Papa."

"I need to think about where Alcida might be, and I cannot do that with anyone else present. I am going into her room, where I shall sit down and try to understand what she might have done. I must do so alone. You can help by shutting yourself inside your bedchamber and calming yourself so that you may think clearly about what she said and did today. Do you understand?"

She nodded. "You want me to imagine I am Miss Blayne so that I can imagine what she might have done and where she might be."

He gave her a hug, delighted, as always, with her quick intelligence. "Exactly. And I shall be doing the same."

Once inside the Indian Room, he walked to the windows where the dark red curtains were drawn back to let in the late afternoon sun. Alcida's work, he was sure. She was made for brightness and light—how dreary she must have found Humber's Harp.

"Papa, Papa!" Clematis's voice roused him from his reverie. "May I come in?"

"Of course."

"I think I know what she did." Clematis pointed to the wainscoting along one of the walls. "She went into the secret passageway right there. She knew about it 'cause I showed her how it opened."

He might have known his inquisitive daughter would have discovered the secrets of Humber's Harp, exactly as he had done as a boy. "I believe you are right," he told her. "You are more quick-witted than I. Open it for me, please."

After she obeyed, he lit a lamp and stepped into the musty, dusty hidden passageway. "You may not follow me," he told her. "Someone must remain behind in case we are wrong and Alcida appears elsewhere."

She nodded.

Alone in the tunnel-like passage, he tried to think what Alcida had in mind. Escape to the Great Hall to slip out the front door unseen? He shook his head. Since she had announced she was leaving, why be clandestine about it? The tower? About to ask himself why she would go there, he slapped his hand against the passage wall. Among a score of scramble-brains, he would win the gudgeon prize. Of course she was in the tower, 'twas as plain as a pikestaff. He ought to have realized that first off.

The tower had been their place. He had brought her there hoping to make love to her and convince her to become his mistress. Instead, he had fallen in love, though God knew he had fought it.

Around and around the passageway curved, always climbing. As he went up and up he heard singing, faint at first, gradually becoming loud enough so the words became intelligible. He knew the singer was Alcida. As he listened to her sweet, clear voice, his heart twisted in his chest:

> My love, my love, is e'er in vain
> He loves me not, nor will he change
> One am I and one will I remain
> My love, my love, is e'er in vain . . .

When at last he reached the top, he searched impatiently for the release, not recalling where it was hidden. He could not find it.

Finally, unable to bear being kept from her side any longer, he shouted through the paneling, "Alcida, my love, Nothing is in vain! Let me in!"

The singing stopped abruptly. For a long moment nothing happened and he prayed she would not, rather than opening to him, flee down the stairs. After an eternity, the panel slid aside. He stepped into the tower and saw her standing there in the drabbest of what he thought of as her governess dresses. Yet she seemed to glow in the dim room. He had never seen a more beautiful woman.

"I don't care who the devil you are," he growled, "you will marry me!"

She stared at him for a moment, her green eyes,

deep and compelling as the sea, wide with shock. Then she blinked and recovered her self-possession. "How do you know I will," she demanded, backing away from his advance, "when you have not yet asked me?"

Driven by an irresistible need to pull her into his arms, already anticipating her eager response to his kiss, he forced himself to hold back. Seeking a way to best express how he felt, he realized he could not find words to tell her what was in his heart.

In desperation, he seized on the words of the song she had been singing and used them to concoct a simple rhyme which he chanted to her:

> If you are one and I am one
> Love is not in vain
> For one and one make two
> And marriage makes us twain.

Her smile carried the warmth of the sun. She opened her arms to him and he swept her into his embrace.

Miles away, Damon walked along the bank of Dane's Run, paying no heed to the flutter of the birds as they flew from bush to tree to bush searching for the ripest berries. He did not hear the murmur of the water, nor the bird calls, nor notice the perfume of the summer flowers mixing with the dank smell of the river. He was aware of nothing but his own dark thoughts.

Ashley was the only woman in the world for him,

there was no denying that fact. She never left his mind, no matter how hard he tried to distract himself. What was he to do about her? His steps slowed and he stopped, staring at the river's flow.

Across, on the other bank, two young rabbits chased each other in circles, either playing or courting, if this *was* the season for rabbits to court. He could not remember. Round and round in circles they hopped, getting neither closer together nor farther apart. Never reaching any conclusion, just like him.

Damn it, he was a man, not a bloody rabbit! Either he had to forget her once and for all, or he must— must *what*?

The answer struck him like a blow, staggering him. He must marry her; it was as simple as that. What did it matter who her parents were? She was Ashley and he loved her.

His surroundings, dull and silent only moments before, suddenly seemed changed. The sun shone warm on his back, birds sang, fish jumped from the water to snap at insects, and the sweet scent of flowers drifted on the breeze.

He turned about and started back to where he had tied his horse. Ashley, he wondered, where are you? The sooner I find you, the sooner we shall be together.

He rounded a bend, and as if his thought had evoked her, he saw Ashley sitting on the bank of Dane's Run with Freddie, who was fishing. He stopped, watching them.

"My thumbs are pricking, Freddie," he heard her say. "Do you know what that means?"

The boy shook his head.

"It means a change is coming, that my life will take another course. Unfortunately, every time it happens, the change never seems to be for the better. What doom do you suppose awaits me now?"

At that moment Freddie looked up and spotted him. Damon put his finger to his lips and Freddie nodded, then handed the pole to Ashley and got to his feet.

"Be back in a bit, I will," he told her, before haring off down the path, away from Damon.

Ashley, watching Freddie dash off, did not turn to look in the other direction. Damon was on her before she either heard him or sensed his presence. She gazed up at him, gasped, and jumped to her feet, dropping the pole. At the same time, a fish took the bait and the pole slid toward the water.

"Look what you have made me do!" she cried. " 'Tis Freddie's new pole." She crouched and made a grab for the pole just as Damon lunged for it. They collided, failed to regain their balance, and like the pole, slid down the bank and plunged into the river.

Sputtering and coughing, Ashley and Damon both surfaced in the shallows and regained their feet. The water, to Damon's calves, rose to her knees. Her flower-sprigged gown clung wetly to her body, revealing every curve. She wrung out her hair, glaring at him all the while.

He grinned at her. "Soon all London will know I have been pushed into Dane's Run by the same innocent maiden as before. What will they make of that?"

"That you take advantage," she snapped.

"Marry me," he said.

She gasped. "What did you say?"

"I believe you heard me. 'Twill not be doom, I promise.

"But I—I mean, you cannot—that is, I cannot—"

"Of course I can, and so can you. Tis simple. I love you. If you love me, all you have to do is say yes. You do love me, don't you?"

"I—I—" she paused and flung her arms around his neck. "Yes, oh yes, Charles, I do."

Freddie's plaintive voice drifted down from the riverbank. "I see ye lost me pole. 'Twas a new pole, but there's no call to drown yerselves going after it."

Wrapped in each other's arms, the two in the water paid him no heed.

Two days later, when the letter came from his solicitor, Roxton opened it, smiling as he read the contents. "We must take this to Lancaster Hall," he said to Alcida, "because it also concerns your sister. I believe the note she sent you yesterday said, among other things, that she was a guest of Lady Lancaster's."

Alcida blinked. "Yes, she is. But what do you mean, the letter also concerns Ashley? Does it then concern me as well?"

He did not answer, saying instead, "Damon is at the Dower House, too. Let us hurry. I cannot wait to share the letter with him."

Alcida had no objections. She was eager to be with her sister, they had been apart far too long. Whatever the solicitor had written was of little importance com-

pared to the wonder of Thomas's love. To observe
proper protocol, Ursula, as Alcida's companion, was
now at Humber's Harp to act as their chaperon until
the wedding. She was delighted about what had come
to pass.

Clematis, equally pleased, took full credit for bringing her father and Alcida together. "For if I had not
remembered about the secret passageway, who knows
what might have happened?" she had insisted.

At Lancaster Hall, the five of them gathered in the
parlor. "We will require the information contained
in this letter for the marriage lines," Roxton said,
"but otherwise . . ." He shrugged. "Of course it will
smooth the twins' acceptance into society."

"What information?" Damon demanded. "I know
you instructed your solicitor to contact the last of the
Winfields as well as this Timothy Jamison, who is handling the twins' legacy. Did anything much come
from it?"

"I am trying to tell you," Roxton said.

Ashley and Alcida, sitting side by side, holding
hands, listened eagerly.

"Ashley and Alcida are the legal offspring of Alyssum, also known as Alice, Winfield and Calvin Livingstone, both deceased."

"Livingstone!" Lady Lancaster and Damon spoke
as one.

"Calvin was killed in a duel, as I recall," Lady Lancaster said. She glanced at the twins. "Sorry to say
he was a scapegrace and a wastrel. The debts he left
drained the family money, and his death broke his

nother's heart. She died less than a year later. His
ather lingered on for another year. If I am correct,
he title went to a cadet branch."

Roxton nodded. "Being female, Ashley and Alcida
have no claim on the title and there is no money to
be had. But the name is legally theirs because Calvin
nd Alyssum were married."

"How did your solicitor ferret that out so quickly?"
Damon asked.

"Old Winfield has the document. He may have dis-
owned his granddaughter, but he got hold of and
kept her marriage lines. We shall try to interest him
n meeting his great-granddaughters—he did not
know they existed."

"Good bloodlines," Lady Lancaster said, beaming
at the twins, "despite the tragedies in both families.
Winfields and Livingstones go way back. You have
nothing to be ashamed of; indeed, if you care to, you
may brag about your ancestry. To think that my in-
terference in your lives brought all this about! It quite
warms my heart."

Ashley looked at Alcida, and without words, each
knew what the other was thinking. What did bloodlines or ancient families matter? They had found one
another, and both were marrying the men they had
given their hearts to, men who had fallen in love with
them and offered for them without knowing or caring what ancestry the twins shared. What more could
anyone ask for?

At the same exact moment, their free hands
reached up to clasp their lockets. Noticing this,
Damon glanced at Roxton and said, "We have successfully unmasked them, ending their masquerade

and sorting out who belongs to whom. Let us hope and pray they have learned a lesson from this. We should be in dire straits, indeed, if they ever decided to confuse us by exchanging lockets!"